I0784978

STARLIGHT AND THE DUKE

The Silver Dukes
Book 5

by

Meara Platt

© Copyright 2025 by Myra Platt
Text by Meara Platt
Cover by Dar Albert

Dragonblade Publishing, Inc. is an imprint of Kathryn Le Veque Novels, Inc.
P.O. Box 23
Moreno Valley, CA 92556
ceo@dragonbladepublishing.com

Produced in the United States of America

First Edition August 2025
Trade Paperback Edition

Reproduction of any kind except where it pertains to short quotes in relation to advertising or promotion is strictly prohibited.

All Rights Reserved.

The characters and events portrayed in this book are fictitious. Any similarity to real persons, living or dead, is purely coincidental and not intended by the author.

ARE YOU SIGNED UP FOR DRAGONBLADE'S BLOG?

You'll get the latest news and information on exclusive giveaways, exclusive excerpts, coming releases, sales, free books, cover reveals and more.

Check out our complete list of authors, too!

No spam, no junk. That's a promise!

Sign Up Here

www.dragonbladepublishing.com

Dearest Reader;

Thank you for your support of a small press. At Dragonblade Publishing, we strive to bring you the highest quality Historical Romance from some of the best authors in the business. Without your support, there is no 'us', so we sincerely hope you adore these stories and find some new favorite authors along the way.

Happy Reading!

CEO, Dragonblade Publishing

Additional Dragonblade books by Author Meara Platt

The Silver Dukes Series
Cherish and the Duke
Moonlight and the Duke
Two Nights with the Duke
Snowfall and the Duke
Starlight and the Duke
Crash Landing on the Duke

The Moonstone Landing Series
Moonstone Landing (Novella)
Moonstone Angel (Novella)
The Moonstone Duke
The Moonstone Marquess
The Moonstone Major
The Moonstone Governess
The Moonstone Hero
The Moonstone Pirate

The Book of Love Series
The Look of Love
The Touch of Love
The Taste of Love
The Song of Love
The Scent of Love
The Kiss of Love
The Chance of Love
The Gift of Love
The Heart of Love
The Hope of Love (Novella)
The Promise of Love
The Wonder of Love

The Journey of Love
The Dream of Love (Novella)
The Treasure of Love
The Dance of Love
The Miracle of Love
The Remembrance of Love (Novella)

Dark Gardens Series
Garden of Shadows
Garden of Light
Garden of Dragons
Garden of Destiny
Garden of Angels

The Farthingale Series
If You Wished For Me (Novella)

The Lyon's Den Series
Kiss of the Lyon
The Lyon's Surprise
Lyon in the Rough

Pirates of Britannia Series
Pearls of Fire

De Wolfe Pack: The Series
Nobody's Angel
Kiss an Angel
Bhrodi's Angel

Also from Meara Platt
Aislin
All I Want for Christmas
Once Upon a Haunted Cave

CHAPTER ONE

London, England
June 1818

"BOLLOCKS, NOT AGAIN," Robert, Duke of Durham, muttered to no one but himself as he stood in the shadows of Lady Forster's terrace, inhaling the scent of lilac in the crisp night air and staring at Lady Fiona Shoreham while she made a cake of herself. He would need to step in and rescue her soon, because even though widowed, she did not know the first thing about men.

Ironic that he was fleeing from entanglements while Fiona was hurling herself back in the marriage game, all because of that betting book at White's that had been started on *him*. The wagers were not on her, for she was a respectable widow with no hint of scandal ever attached to her name. For this reason, no one was particularly interested in her prospects despite the fact that she was charming and beautiful.

"Oh, Lord Dexter," Fiona said with a tense laugh, "mind your step and try not to stumble into me. We are only out here for a moment of fresh air."

Dexter, that sot, chortled. "My apologies, my little dove."

Rob's stomach churned, for Fiona should not be out in this moonlit garden with anyone but him. *He* was the one the *ton* was wagering on, for the sole reason they needed something to relieve their boredom. After the downfall of the latest Silver Duke—Jonas, Duke of Ramsdale—they had turned their attention toward the man they considered London's next most eligible bachelor, and that honor happened to fall on *him*.

Bets were now being taken on when he would marry, and which fortunate lady he would choose, even though he did not quite meet the qualifications of a Silver Duke.

But he was a duke and unmarried, hence the frenzy.

He also had a dusting of silver at his temples now that he had turned two and thirty, and this added to the unwarranted attention heaped on him. Apparently, mere flecks of silver in one's hair was enough to qualify one for that elevated status.

The irony of it all was too bitter to swallow, and he did not want to think beyond the need to step in and protect Fiona from a drunken Lord Dexter when he proved to be no gentleman. "Gad, Fiona. Move away from that clot," he said in a whisper, watching as Dexter began to make a move on her.

Good thing Robert had ensconced himself in this darkened spot to escape the crush of Lady Forster's ever-popular Midsummer Ball. What he was really escaping were the hunters, those predatory debutantes one might mistake for charming innocents clad in finest silks and lacy gloves, dripping pearls from their ears and delicate throats. But they were lethal predators who sought him out bearing coquettish smiles, their eagle eyes trained on him to mark him as their next prey.

The only reason they now hunted him down was because he had inherited one of the most respected and powerful dukedoms in England, becoming the twelfth Duke of Durham as of a month ago. This was proving to be a bloody nuisance. Why did he have to be the *twelfth* in the proud and venerable line? The title came with a ridiculous amount of wealth along with the power that he could wield as irresponsibly as he wished, short of treasonous actions against the Crown, and no one would stop him.

Which also led him to another reason he stood apart from the overly perfumed, sweating bodies in the ballroom. Being a duke also meant he could no longer put off the inevitable and seek a wife.

This was a problem because Fiona was the only woman he

had ever wanted…and the only woman who refused to have him.

Which explained why she was at this moment seated on a bench beside the garden fountain fluttering her fan and eyelashes at that sotted goat, the Earl of Dexter, laughing inanely at his dull conversation.

"Stop, Fiona," he muttered, recognizing the dangerous leer on Dexter's face and knowing it meant trouble.

Robert had to save Fiona, of course.

They had been friends all of his life, even before he was old enough to retain memories, which happened for him at around the age of three. There she was, from his earliest recollections, smiling at him with her sparkling aquamarine eyes, and those dark, springy curls that surrounded her sweet face seeming to take on a life of their own as they bounced around her ears.

To this day, her smile was so radiant, one might believe she had swallowed the sun.

What a bloody fool he was.

He started down the terrace steps toward her the moment he noticed Dexter's hand begin to slide to her pert, rounded bottom.

Fiona realized it at the same moment and playfully slapped Dexter's hand away with her fan. "Now, now, my lord," she said, emitting a nervous trill of laughter. "You mustn't."

But, of course, Dexter was going to try again, and a little slap on the wrist was not going to deter him.

Fiona had never understood men and their baser urges.

Robert hurried his pace, for he knew where Dexter's desires were aimed next, and he would have to kill the man if he set a hand on Fiona's body. "Is there a problem, Lady Shoreham?"

"Mind your own business," an obviously foxed Lord Dexter growled, his face distorted by the golden flames of torchlight that surrounded the fountain and cast his features in a menacing glow.

"I suggest you keep your hands to yourself," Robert growled back, his own curling into fists at his sides.

He saw relief wash over Fiona's face as she broke away from the drunken lord and fled to his side. "I would like to go back inside now," she said in a strained whisper that was almost drowned out by the lilting chords of a waltz filtering into the garden from the ballroom.

Robert offered his arm and led her back toward the house, but stopped as they were about to climb the terrace steps that led into the crowded ballroom. "Need I say it?"

She looked up at him, her features easily discerned because not only torchlight filled the garden on this summer evening. The night sky was almost cloudless, one of those rare skies where one could see the diamond sparkle of starlight against an ink-black emptiness, and silver moonlight under the moon's crescent glow.

"You are angry with me, aren't you?" Fiona asked. "I can feel the tension in your muscles."

He let out a breath of frustration. "What in blazes are you thinking? Do you have no clue what impression you are giving Dexter and every other dolt you flirt with?"

She tipped her chin up. "I made it quite clear to Lord Dexter that we were only to take a turn about the garden and nothing more. *Nothing* more."

He rolled his eyes. "Oh, of course. And you expect him to believe this is all you want when you flutter and chirp and *smile* at him?"

"What is wrong with my smile?"

Nothing, other than it was achingly beautiful.

"He's drunk, and you think he did not take your flirtations and fluttering fan as signals of something more?"

She huffed. "I did not do anything with my fan other than use it as a weapon to swat his hand away. Rest assured, I would have shoved it up one or another of his orifices had he not taken the hint. How dare you reprimand me."

Robert stared at her incredulously. "How dare I? Fine, I'll let the next oaf manhandle you and won't interfere. Fight him off on your own."

"I shall do so quite capably without your interference."

"Is that so?" He grunted in exasperation. "Then fight off as many of those old buzzards as you wish, for I will not stop them anymore."

He turned to walk away, but she held him back. "All right, it was stupid of me. I admit it, Rob. Thank you for coming to my rescue. I sincerely appreciate it."

He let out a breath. "Why did you do it, Fiona?"

"Because…"

"Oh, that is an excellent explanation," he said after a prolonged stretch of silence between them. "That clarifies everything for me. *Because.* That is a completely understandable motive."

She pinched his forearm. "Do not be insufferable. I did it for you, as you ought to know by now."

He felt a lurch in the pit of his stomach because he did know, and the reason was inescapable.

I did it for you.

She had done it for his sake because she knew he would never move on from loving her unless she were no longer available.

She had done it to him once—not her fault. How was an eighteen-year-old girl ever to pay attention to an eleven-year-old boy who was on the cusp of turning twelve? Nor would he ever have thought to stop the Earl of Shoreham from marrying Fiona when he had no idea of the damage it was about to do to his own heart.

That damnable six-year age difference between them was insurmountable back then.

But now?

His frustration returned, for she still believed it was insurmountable and he was too young for her, even though he was a man full grown and in his early thirties.

A man who knew what love meant and what it felt like, that inability to breathe around this woman who radiated sparkle and sunshine.

He hated the irony of it.

While every other woman in England wanted him, thought he was sinfully handsome, and was desperate to have him, Fiona still saw him as the toddler whose bottom she had powdered when he was the age of two. And whose bloodied knees and elbows she had tended when he had fallen out of an apple tree when he was seven.

Or whose wounds she had nursed when he returned from the Napoleonic War, shipped home before the final, decisive battles because he was too injured and battered to participate.

She had not hesitated to care for and protect him as she had done all of her life, for he and Fiona had grown up as neighbors and their mothers had been best friends, which constantly threw them in each other's company.

For this reason, he and Fiona had never lost touch.

And now she was determined to marry some worthless clot because *he*—the duke that every other woman in England wanted—would never marry while she remained available.

He understood the logic of her reasoning and was infuriated by it. "Do not ruin your life simply thinking to save mine," he said with a growl.

She frowned at him. "Why not?"

"It won't work and you'll only make yourself miserable."

"I won't."

"Fiona, you will."

She sighed. "You are the most stubborn person I know."

He frowned back. "Oh, no. You are."

"No, you are."

They laughed at the same moment, for they both sounded like children.

"Truce?" she asked.

He nodded, although he had no intention of giving up on her. It would be a different matter entirely if she truly did not care for him. But what had once been a true friendship had turned recently into something more.

Something far deeper.

There was heat between them, and not only coming from him. She felt those fiery sparks as much as he did.

Dexter lumbered up the terrace steps past them, pausing to toss Fiona an angry and insulting look.

Rob was about to step forward to wipe the insolence off the drunken sot's face, but Fiona put her hand back on his arm. "He isn't worth it."

"I could have told you that before you ever walked out of the ballroom with him," he grumbled, knowing he was being unfair to her.

"Are you done scolding me?"

He let out a breath and nodded. "Just do me a favor and stop encouraging those clots."

"Then you must do me a favor and *start* encouraging those debutantes."

It wasn't going to happen. And Fiona knew him well enough to see the refusal in his eyes.

"So this is how you are going to play your hand, is it?" She peered into the ballroom. "Ah, there's Lord Wilton. He's recently widowed. I think I shall go forward and throw myself at him."

"Damn it, Fiona. Don't."

"How are you going to stop me?"

With a kiss, came to mind.

A hot, toe-curling, swallow-each-other-up sort of kiss that scorched one's soul into eternity.

He'd been wanting to do this for months already.

She saw the heat in his eyes and groaned. "Rob, we cannot go on like this."

"Like what? Never touching each other and pretending we are not meant for each other? There's an easy remedy."

"Yes, there is. But it is not what you are thinking."

He was thinking marriage, and she knew it.

"I have a proposition for you," she said slowly.

He was willing to listen to any idea that would bring them together. "Go on."

She looked up at him with her big aquamarine eyes and casually brushed back a dark curl that had loosened from its pin and was now dancing against her ear in the night breeze.

This was why he found it impossible to move on. She still glowed with an inner beauty that would never fade. Her smile was shimmering starlight.

He could teach her so many things, if only she would let him. But he wanted to teach her as her husband, show her how to let her passion flow as he knew she had never done with her late husband, Lord Albert Shoreham.

This was part of the problem.

Her husband had been a good man and devoted to her, but he was about as exciting as a limp dishcloth. As improbable as it may be, Rob did not think Shoreham had ever…

The point was, Fiona did not know what true passion or arousal were. He could not even imagine what those two had done between the sheets. Clothes were probably kept on at all times.

In truth, he did not want to know.

"Here's the proposition," she said, clearing her throat. "You want me."

Had he not made this abundantly clear?

"But you only *think* you do." She sighed. "You only want me because I have been a challenge."

"I want you," he said with insistence, "because you are what my heart needs."

She regarded him in that stubborn, pursed-lips way again. "You need to move on and marry someone suitable, someone young and vital who can share a lifetime with you."

How was this not her?

But he knew the rest of it, the Sword of Damocles hanging over her head that she was not expressing. The quiet despair and impending sense of doom she always felt because, in all their years of marriage, she and Shoreham had never had children.

She blamed herself.

Rob blamed no one. Some things just were what they were— no fault to lay at anyone's feet. Not hers or Shoreham's.

"Tell me the rest of it," he prodded when she did not immediately continue.

She took a deep breath, no doubt finding their situation as difficult as he did. "You need to get over me and find yourself the next Duchess of Durham. So, get over me."

"What?"

"Get on top of me. Under me."

He choked out a cough. "What?"

"Come up to Shoreham Manor a week before Gawain and Cherish's summer house party begins…and share my bed."

"Fiona." His heart broke, for he knew where she was going with this.

"You shall have me to yourself for the entire week, and then you can simply ride next door to join Gawain and Cherish at Northam Hall, no one the wiser."

"You think they will not know I have just spent a week with you beforehand?"

"My servants would never talk."

Yes, they would. Perhaps not to the outside world, but they would blab all to the Northam Hall staff, many of whom were related to the staff at Shoreham Manor, since they were neighboring properties, not to mention Fiona and Cherish were as close as sisters.

However, Rob was not going to fight about it. He wanted to hear the rest of her doomed-to-failure plan.

"A week with you," she continued, refusing to see the impending disaster of her idea, "and then we can pretend we are just meeting the following week at Cherish's house party. Perhaps I'll merely ride over daily, not participate too much in order to give you time with the young ladies they have invited."

"No, Fiona. I'm sure Cherish has invited you to stay over for the duration of her party. She'll expect it of you and question your reasons if you don't. Besides, it isn't safe for you to be traveling home every night after supper or whatever events they have planned."

"I'll think about it," she said with a nod to acknowledge his point about the dangers lurking in the wee hours. "No need to make a decision on that yet. Gawain is my cousin and Cherish is my best friend. If I need a room, they will accommodate me."

But Rob wished to know more about this proposal of hers. Offering to spend a week in bed with him *had* to come with strings attached. "And what is the price I am to pay for this week-long frolic in your bed?"

"Cherish has invited several young ladies to her house party, all of them lovely and more than suitable to be your duchess. Once the party begins, you must promise to give each one serious consideration."

"That's it?"

"No." She took a deep breath. "And you must promise to choose one of them to be your bride by the end of the house party."

"That is no bargain," he grumbled.

Fiona held up a hand. "Do not be so hasty to refuse, for there is no other sensible solution. You shall have me, all of me, *before* they arrive. An entire week alone with me to get me out of your system."

His heart was not a *system*.

She cast him a pleading look. "Don't you see? It is your unfulfilled fantasies that are the problem, Rob. So I am giving you permission to fulfill them."

"Full access to your body?"

And your heart, Fiona. It is your heart that I want.

She cleared her throat again. "Yes, full access. What do you say? Does this proposal meet with your approval?"

No, it was a terrible idea. Incredibly foolish. He would have to be out of his mind to accept.

But he nodded. "Yes, let's do it."

CHAPTER TWO

FIONA'S SMILE FALTERED as she felt the impact of Rob's smoldering gaze on her. It tore through her like wildfire. And now he was nodding and agreeing to… *Dear heaven*, what was she thinking? This was going to be a disaster.

He rubbed a hand across the nape of his neck. "I am accepting your proposal with one modification."

They were still standing on the steps of Lady Forster's terrace, the lively strains of a popular English reel filling the night air. He looked magnificent in his black tie and tails, his jacket cut to perfection and stretching with impeccable precision across his broad shoulders before molding to his muscled torso and trim waist. "What modification?"

His eyes were the most stunning shade of green she had ever beheld, reminiscent of an emerald ocean and flecked with silver, as though he had captured the stars and they now shone only through him.

This was what made his gaze so dangerous. One glance was all it took, and he had her insides tumbling like a capsized boat upon rough waters.

His dark-gold hair also had flecks of silver at the temples, which gave him an aura of authority to add to his already too-tempting features.

However, as dangerously handsome as Rob was, she knew that she would always be safe with him.

Always.

He gave her cheek a light caress. "I am not going to propose to anyone until three months after the house party."

Pain filled her, for she understood the reason for his caution. He thought their activities in the week before the house party might leave her with child.

What a painful jest. Did he not understand what it meant to be barren? This was what she was, and had almost twenty years of empty hopes to prove it.

He should not have raised the issue when he knew how much it upset her. How could she ever fulfill the *only* requirement vital to becoming his duchess, the ability to produce an heir? He knew this and stubbornly refused to accept it.

His arms came around her and he hugged her to him as she struggled to regain her composure. "Three months, Rob? Why bother? You know there is no chance of my conceiving." She emitted a ragged sigh, for every word carried a wealth of ache.

"We'll see."

"Stop, Rob. I know how protective you are of me, but not even you can fix this. Neither your *potency* nor your prowess in the bedchamber is going to fix me. No more talk about this, please. I need to pull myself together before I walk back into the ballroom."

He regarded her with obvious reluctance. "All right, but do you really want to return inside?"

"It is almost midnight and they will soon ring the bell for supper."

"Are you hungry?"

She gave a curt laugh. "Not in the least."

"Shall I take you home?" He was being gentle with her again, as he always was. "Or have you brought your own carriage?"

She shook her head. "I came with Cherish and Gawain."

She had never been happier than when Cherish had married Fiona's cousin, Gawain, Duke of Bromleigh, one of the *ton's* notorious Silver Dukes until tamed by Cherish. Fiona was proud to have brought about their love match.

If only the same were possible for herself.

But she'd had her turn at marriage and harbored no regrets, for Shoreham had been a good husband on the whole. Theirs had never been a passionate love match, but a very good and caring friendship.

That made for a successful marriage, did it not?

"Let me find Bromleigh," Rob said, his voice a deep rumble that flowed through her like warm honey. "I'll let him know I am taking you home."

"You needn't."

"I know, but do you want to remain at this party?"

She shook her head, feeling a sudden chill that sprang from her insides and not from the crisp night air surrounding them. "No."

He placed her arm in his and led her inside, steering her through the crush and into the entry hall. He asked for his carriage to be brought around, and then turned to her. "Wait here. I'll advise Bromleigh I am taking you home. I'll be right back."

She nodded, suddenly feeling quite alone even though footmen were scurrying all around her and some of the partygoers had spilled out of the ballroom into this front hall. She smiled at a few when they acknowledged her. Spoke briefly to one or two of them. But she always felt an emptiness when Robert Durham left her side, even now as he left briefly to convey a message to her cousin.

She hated this need for him, and how desperately her heart had grown to crave him.

In every other respect, she was capable, confident, and enjoyed her independence. She liked being in charge and managing her own assets, for her dear Shoreham had been generous in providing for her. She also liked meddling in other people's affairs, especially when it came to romantic matters. She was very good at making love matches, Gawain and Cherish being perhaps her greatest achievement.

But this was why being around Rob unsettled her so much.

If such a thing as mates of the heart existed, he was hers.

And perhaps this was why she was sabotaging her own efforts to remarry, always choosing to flirt with clots like Lord Dexter because she could never take them seriously and would never be so foolish as to marry such a man.

There was only one man she wanted, and that was Robert Durham.

But he needed a wife who could produce an heir.

This failing in her might not have mattered had he a slew of siblings, namely brothers, or even male cousins who could have taken on the responsibility of siring Durham male heirs. But Rob was the last. The title would extinguish upon his death, leaving at risk all his remaining relatives, most of whom were elderly ladies and utterly dependent on him to maintain their genteel lives. He also had employees, tenants, servants, and so many others who were under his protection and needed this proud line to continue.

That he would choose her above all his duties overwhelmed and humbled her, but they both knew it was wrong.

Rob strode out of the ballroom and cast her a smile as he approached. "Gawain is duly advised. Let's get you home."

She smothered a grin as the impressive Durham carriage rolled up in front of the Forster residence. It was as big and powerful as its owner, its black steel gleaming in the torchlight and the rampant lions on the Durham crest emblazoned on the door looking ready to leap out and devour her.

Rob helped her climb in, lightly wrapping his hands around her waist to give her the slight boost. She sat on the forward-facing bench seat and watched Rob settle into the seat across from hers, leaning his broad shoulders against the soft leather squabs.

"How does it feel to be a duke now?" she asked, for they had not seen each other much in the months leading up to his inheritance of the title. He looked quite big within the confines of the carriage.

And quite daunting.

"I don't mind the added work. In fact, I am enjoying it. But I detest the attention."

"You have always had the ability to command a room, with or without your title. People always notice you." Because he carried himself with an elegant grace, moving about a ballroom with the confidence of a panther on the prowl.

He was giving her that panther look now, those shimmering eyes trained on her as they rode along the familiar London streets that were eerily quiet at this hour. All she could hear was the *clop-clop* of the carriage horses as their hooves hit the ground, and the squeak of carriage springs as they jounced along.

She blushed under the force of his stare. Shivers of delight ran through her despite her efforts to ignore the raw heat of him. "I am going to jump out of your carriage if you continue to look at me this way."

"How am I looking at you?" Even his voice held power, for it was deep, smooth, and dangerous.

"You are already imagining me in your bed."

He shrugged. "You are the one who suggested it. Having second thoughts?"

"No." Giving him full access to her body was the perfect solution, and they both knew it. He would satisfy his fantasies and move on.

She would satisfy *hers*. An entire week with Rob to give her memories to dream on. Hot, set-fire-to-the-bed memories to warm her lonely nights.

And why not?

She noticed his hands, big and slightly roughened because he was no dandy. She noticed his smile, the way it shone through his silver-flecked eyes and seemed meant just for her. Most of all, she loved the quiet seriousness about him, a trait he'd displayed even as a child, an innate confidence and assurance that instilled trust in all who knew him.

A week seemed a proper length of time for both of them to get what they needed from each other and move on.

"Would you like to come in for a cup of tea?" she asked when they had arrived at her elegant townhouse in Duchess Square, one of those lovely Mayfair enclaves lined with pretty trees and blooming flowers, particularly wisteria in April and May, and roses throughout the summer. "We can discuss this plan further, if you wish. Or do nothing of the sort and simply chat about things in general."

"Not tonight, Fiona."

She swallowed her disappointment, for she had not expected him to refuse her invitation.

He led her to the door and watched as she turned the latch-key to let herself into her home. There was no butler on duty at this late hour to open it for her, nor would she ever assign anyone on her staff to such a duty, forcing them to stay awake for hours when she was fully capable of letting herself in.

Rob entered with her and made certain nothing was amiss before turning to leave. "Lock that door after me."

"Yes, sir," she replied with military curtness, then smiled because she loved that protective quality about him.

He would make a good husband and father someday. Those protective instincts were very strong in him. Yet he would never be overbearing or demanding.

"Will I see you tomorrow, Rob?"

"No."

"Oh." She had been invited to supper at Cherish's home. Gawain's friends, Lynton, Camborne, and Ramsdale, were to join them with their wives. The four men had been considered Silver Dukes, handsome, fortyish, dashes of silver at the temples, and confirmed bachelors until meeting the women who had won their hearts.

But if Rob was not to be there, then would she be the odd female in their numbers?

"Reggie will probably attend the supper party to even out the table," he said, reading her thoughts. "Margaret is visiting her parents this week, so he'll attend on his own."

Lord Reginald Burton was Gawain's nephew and Rob's best friend. He was also related to Fiona, a first cousin once removed, if one were to adhere to the precise terms for lines of descent and consanguinity. Reggie was a good soul and would be excellent company. "And you? Did they not invite you?"

"They did. But I have Durham business matters that need my attention. I'll be leaving for Devonshire first thing tomorrow morning."

"When will you be back in London?"

"I won't. It doesn't make sense for me to return here just to turn around and head back south for Cherish and Gawain's summer party."

"So you'll join me at Shoreham Manor a week before their party begins? I am serious about my proposal, Rob. It is the only sensible solution for us."

"It is hardly sensible," he muttered, but cast her a rakish grin. "Nor am I likely to forget that invitation to join you in your bed. I never took you for a wanton, Fiona."

She gasped. "I am no such thing!"

He arched an eyebrow. "Admit it, you are eager for my body."

"It is a selfless act of sacrifice and nothing more," she said, frowning at him.

"If you say so, Joan of Arc." He leaned forward and gave her a chaste kiss on the forehead.

She smothered her disappointment, wishing he might have kissed her on the lips now that they had struck this scandalous bargain.

But Rob was too noble ever to take advantage. Since their week of tawdry lusting had not yet started, he would remain a gentleman.

Though perhaps her disappointment had not been all that smothered, since he now regarded her with bone-melting heat.

"Gad, Fiona."

"What?"

He cast her a smug grin. "You want me."

She punched his shoulder. "Go away, Durham. You are irritating me."

He cast her that I'm-a-hungry-panther-about-to-devour-you look. "Good night, Fiona."

He turned around and walked out the door. She closed it and then leaned her entire body against it, her knees too weak to hold her up.

Dear heaven.

Even her breaths were ragged.

How could this happen?

Her head was still resting against the door when she suddenly heard a sharp rap that had her leaping to attention. "Fiona, lock that door."

Was Rob still here?

"I am not leaving until I know that latch has fallen into place."

"Doing it right now," she assured him, and hastily complied. "Did you hear that? All done. I'm safe. See you in a few weeks."

But there was a heavy silence on the other side of the door.

She knew he was still there because she felt him. This was what happened whenever he was close—her skin prickled and she felt alive.

"I will see you then, won't I?"

Still silence.

He wasn't having a change of heart, was he?

CHAPTER THREE

Shoreham Manor
Near Brighton, England
July, 1818

ROB ABSENTLY GAZED out the window as his carriage rolled past Brighton and the familiar patches of seacoast along the countryside. His heart beat a little faster, for Fiona's home, Shoreham Manor, was not far from here.

Not that he had been counting the days, hours, or minutes until seeing her again.

But he had been.

The familiar house came into view and he edged forward, eager to see Fiona's smiling face. Were they really going to do this? Hot, lustful, naked sex for a week?

Fiona, for all her brashness, was quite shy when it came to matters of the boudoir. Perhaps not shy, exactly, but in many ways ignorant of all that could go on between the sheets. Despite her streak of independence, she was also quite traditional.

She could be quite proper when she wanted to be.

His heart opened up when he saw her standing by the door, all smiles and bobbing, dark curls as she caught sight of his carriage and waved to him.

He waved in response, then eased back and emitted a groaning breath. "What are we doing to each other, Fiona?" he muttered.

This was the question he had asked himself repeatedly over the last three weeks, ever since she had proposed the idea. A thousand times he'd asked himself this question and never came up with answers.

He remained plagued by doubts. How could he spend a week in Fiona's bed, explore her body with shocking intimacy, and then just leave her to marry someone else?

Only the vilest of rakehells would ever do such a thing, and he had never been a rake or such a cad of a man.

The simple answer was that he could not abandon her in this fashion.

But he was not going to say anything to Fiona just yet. She had to feel this impossibility for herself.

He hoped by the time their week was up and the Bromleighs' house party guests began to arrive, she would understand their hearts, souls, and bodies were never meant to be apart.

He hopped down as soon as his driver drew the team to a halt in front of the rambling country house surrounded by an abundance of red roses and wildflowers. It was everything a country house ought to be, old but well maintained, large but still possessing a quiet charm. A cozy retreat that felt like heaven because this was where Fiona resided.

"How have you been, Lady Shoreham?" he asked, striding toward her. He always kept to formality whenever in the presence of others, even if it was only that of her butler, Simmons.

"I am excellent, Durham," she replied, also addressing him with proper formality. "How did your Devonshire business go?"

"Smoothly. I finished faster than expected and hope you won't mind my imposing on you a week early?"

Fiona had contrived this stupid charade that was not going to fool anyone on her staff, especially not Simmons or her capable housekeeper, Mrs. Harris. Nor would this contrived excuse ever fool Gawain, the Duke of Bromleigh, or his wife, Cherish, who owned the neighboring property, Northam Hall.

He did not know if they had opened their seaside house yet or were still in London. However, since their house party was only a week away, they would have to return here to open the house within the next day or two.

What would Fiona do if Cherish strolled over one morning and found him already ensconced here?

Well, that was Fiona's problem. He was ready to marry her if her honor was ever placed in question.

She locked her arm in his and led him into the house. "Come onto the terrace with me while Mrs. Harris prepares your guest quarters. There's a lovely breeze off the water. Simmons will bring up your bags. We'll have time to share a lemonade before you head upstairs to freshen up."

"That will be welcome," he said, for his throat was dry. It wasn't from the ride, for he had spent last night at a comfortable inn not far from here. It was located in one of those charming coastal villages only about four hours west of Brighton.

The weather this morning had been dry and beautiful, allowing him to make quick time in his travels. But the sight of Fiona, her dark curls in a jumble and her smile as dazzling as ever, had tightened his throat with an all-too-familiar longing.

She still had the exuberance of a girl approaching womanhood, and her body had not changed all that much in the twenty years since her wedding day. She was perhaps a little fuller in the bosom and a touch broader in the hips, but still slender and full of vigor. And that sweet face of hers, so lively and welcoming. Was there anyone prettier?

Mrs. Harris served them their lemonade and dutifully expressed that she was pleased to see him. They exchanged quick pleasantries before she scrambled off to finish her work.

"You have a good staff. They seem to be taking excellent care of you."

"They are, and they like you, too. They think you are my nicest and politest guest."

This came as no surprise, since he had been here often enough over the years, and was always on his best behavior. In fact, Fiona's staff often turned to him for assistance when some of her other guests turned loutish during her own popular summer house parties. Tempers could flare when the weather turned sour and there was little to do other than drink. He was always the one to keep matters from getting out of hand.

Surprisingly, this had happened even when Shoreham was alive. He'd always stepped in to help, for Shoreham was a gentle soul and did not have the physical build to grab a hotheaded drunkard by the nape and toss him outdoors to cool off.

"Fiona, have you planned anything for us today?"

"No," she said with a shake of her head. "I wasn't certain you would show up."

"Still, you dressed for me. You look very pretty." She had on a gown of palest pink muslin that seemed to brighten the bluish-green swirls of her eyes and put a blush on her cheeks.

"Oh, this old thing?" She glanced down and patted her hair with a feigned casual air.

He leaned forward and grinned. "Yes, that *old* thing which happens to be in the latest style of fashion. Not to mention, I have never seen you wear it before."

"Oh, haven't you? How odd. Well, I suppose we haven't seen much of each other lately, have we? But as for this afternoon's plans, as I said, I've made none for us, since I wasn't certain when or if you would arrive."

She glanced up at the sky. "It is a spectacular day and should not be wasted indoors. We could have a picnic lunch on the beach. Does this meet with your approval?"

He nodded. "Great idea. The shadows will be starting to stretch along the sand within the hour and provide shade if we sit by the stairs. We can take a walk along the beach after we eat, if you don't mind. I could do with stretching my legs a bit."

"Sounds perfect."

She escorted him upstairs once his room was declared ready. It was inconveniently located at the opposite end of the hall from hers. For the sake of propriety, of course. Still, it gave him some concern, since he would be forced to come and go from her bedchamber using the hallway. There was a risk he would be seen by a passing servant.

Well, they would figure out a solution later.

Not that it mattered. Fiona wore her feelings on her sleeve. Everyone would know by the satisfied glow on her face once he had bedded her.

Nor was he being full of himself to think he could make her quiver with passion. He could do it because of the strong bond of affection that already existed between them.

As for him, all she had to do was smile and he was lost.

He used the ewer of fresh water and its matching basin to wash the dirt off his face and body, then put on fresh clothes before returning downstairs. Since they were heading down to the beach, he did not bother to don a jacket or cravat. A linen shirt, buff trousers, and walking boots would do.

Fiona had not changed out of her pink muslin gown, but now wore a large straw hat trimmed with a matching pink silk ribbon to protect her skin from the sun.

He liked her in that hat, which was far prettier than a bonnet that would hide her face and dull her eyes. But under this hat, her eyes were big and bright.

"Shall we go?" she asked.

He grabbed the picnic basket and nodded. "Lead the way."

She took the blanket Mrs. Harris now handed her.

They said nothing to each other, nor did they exchange a touch or look, while they made their way along the path and down the steps to the beach.

Nevertheless, sparks flew between them. Rob knew she had to be feeling these same jolts of excitement.

Perhaps their lunch was not the only thing he would taste while on the beach. He longed to put his mouth on hers and taste the sweetness of her lips. He ached to put his mouth anywhere on her body she would allow, for he had always adored her scent, which was never stale or overly perfumed but always fresh and natural as newly picked apples.

But he would wait and see what Fiona wanted. This week was not about sex, but love.

Although the path to love was going to be through having sex with her.

If Fiona thought they would have their fill of each other by rutting like rabbits and then be done, she was naïve. He meant to make their lovemaking hot and shattering. His plan was to turn himself into an essential need for her, one she could no more do without than air in her lungs.

But today was not a day for action. Reconnaissance first. Check out the territory.

A gentle summer breeze shimmered through the lush foliage and relaxed him as they walked along the lightly wooded path toward the beach.

However, Rob could tell Fiona was tense. "Are you all set for Cherish and Gawain's house party? Are there any chores I can help you with? I know you and Cherish often help each other out whether it is your party or hers."

She smiled as their path emerged onto a grassy expanse that led to the beach steps. "She'll let me know if there is anything more I can do for her. I've already helped with the invitations and the general planning, so I think she'll be prepared. Organization is one of my strengths. I also came ahead to make certain her house was fully stocked and that daily deliveries of perishable goods have been arranged, and I helped her write a schedule of daily activities and alternative plans in the event of rain."

He laughed. "Is this her house party or yours?"

She shrugged. "I love this sort of thing. She knows I am here to help if something comes up that she needs me to do."

"You are a good and loyal friend to her. A good friend to me, as well."

He'd meant to compliment her, but saw pain in her fragile smile. "Always, Rob. I shall always hold you dearest in my heart."

"Same here," he replied, his voice tight. "You know that, don't you?"

She smiled at him and nodded.

They walked on in silence, but then both came to a sudden stop as they reached the beach steps. From here, one had a magnificent view of Shoreham Manor's sheltered cove and the sunlight glistening upon the gentle waves.

Rob took a deep breath, for there was something quite bracing about the salty sea air. "Would you mind if I took a swim later?"

Fiona shrugged. "Not at all. I might dip my toes in the water while you have your swim."

He arched an eyebrow. "You could join me."

She blushed. "I don't think so. I am not as strong a swimmer as you. Besides, I did not think to put on my bathing costume."

He left it at that as they walked down the stairs onto the sand and spread the blanket within the shade of the steps. Fiona opened the picnic basket and set out what was packed inside— cold ham, cheese, and bread.

"Looks delicious," he remarked.

She nodded. "I have a good staff. They take excellent care of me."

When they were done with their repast, they removed their boots and walked barefoot along the sand. Rob purposely did not touch Fiona, not even to take her hand. He could see that she was still fragile, for his presence alone was forcing her to face her feelings, and this was difficult for her.

But it was better that they dealt with this turmoil now.

If Fiona had helped Cherish send out her invitations, then most of the young ladies who were invited had no doubt been chosen for him by Fiona.

How would she handle seeing him in the company of these potential wives? He did not think she was capable of remaining indifferent.

What a mess this was going to be.

As they ambled back toward the blanket and the beach steps, he stopped to roll up the legs of his trousers.

Fiona watched him. "What are you doing?"

"Dipping a toe in the water. Care to join me for that? It is innocent enough."

Nodding, she hiked her gown up to her knees and ventured into the water alongside him. He liked watching her dance amid the waves, darting forward and then back as they gently broke around her. What a beautiful portrait she made with her big eyes shining under that big, floppy hat, its pink ribbon fluttering in the wind.

Her legs were nicely shaped, too. He'd never seen more than her ankles in almost twenty years. But in their earlier days, when they were children, he'd seen her legs lots of times, for they often climbed trees or hopped fences, her long, spindly limbs flailing as she struggled to lift herself up.

Fiona had never had much upper body strength. She made it up a tree or over a fence by sheer determination.

"I'm going in for a swim," he said, tugging his shirt out of his waistband. "Turn around, Fiona. I'm taking everything off."

A hot blush stained her cheeks, but she did not turn away. Instead, she tipped her chin into the air. "What difference does it make? I'm going to see you *that* way eventually, aren't I?"

"Yes, but only when you are ready and willing. I have no intention of rushing you into anything."

She swallowed hard but did not take her gaze off him.

"Fine, pretend you are jaded and sophisticated." He removed his shirt in one fluid motion and held back a chuckle when he heard her make a strangled sound, halfway between a kitten's meow and a bird chirp, because she wasn't used to seeing bared muscles or broad shoulders on a man. Her late husband was built more like a slender willow reed.

"All right, Fiona. Moment of truth. I'm taking off my trousers now. Are you going to stay stubborn and gawk at me? Pretend you are not going to silently shriek and panic? Or will you turn your back? Do it now." He stared at her while undoing the first button of his falls, then the second.

Her face turned a brighter shade of red as she spun around to stare at the beach steps. "I am only looking away to protect your modesty."

"Mine? I am not modest. Turn around if you want to look at me. I know you are dying of curiosity. But it will also be a shock to your senses."

She huffed. "Pardon me while I yawn."

Laughing, he took off his trousers and dove into the bracing sea.

"You can look now," he called out once the water was above his waist. The water was clear, although hopefully roiled enough by the small waves breaking around him so as not to give her too much of a view. She wanted to appear brave, but in fact she was a skittish filly.

Perhaps he was treating her too much like an innocent, but this was what she was to some degree. She was not sophisticated about sexual matters, although she probably assumed she was, due to her almost twenty-year marriage.

But what had she and Shoreham done in all those years? It was clear to Rob that she understood almost nothing about men's bodies. Shoreham had been her one and only, and obviously taught her very little. Nor had anyone touched her before marriage or after she'd lost her husband.

Was he being a prideful arse by worrying about showing her too much *maleness* all at once?

Fiona was no wilting daffodil. She wasn't going to swoon or faint at the evidence of his masculinity.

But she was a thinker, and this was what she was going to do—think too much and then obsess over every detail.

She turned to watch him in the water and was now staring at him with the intensity of the sun.

Obviously, she was contemplating joining him.

"The water is quite splendid, Fiona."

When she did not respond, he let the matter drop and swam the length of the cove and back. She probably studied his arse, the very same one she had powdered when he was a toddler.

One's arse did not change much from infancy to adulthood. It was the package up front that mattered most.

"Look away, Fiona. I'm coming out now."

"I don't see why I should."

"Are we going to play this game again?" He brushed back his wet hair to keep it off his face. "Fine, don't turn around. Show me how comfortable you are around a man's naked body. Because I am *very* naked, Fiona."

And he knew she wasn't comfortable at all. Shoreham must have come to her bundled to his throat.

"This final warning is a courtesy to you. As for myself, I don't care if you look your fill."

But he had not waded more than a step forward before she made another of those chirping bird sounds and turned away. She did not move away from his pile of clothing, however.

He stepped out of the water and closed the distance between them, bending to retrieve the trousers by her feet. Water dripped from his hair and body, and a little of it fell on her as he shook himself like a dog to wipe the excess moisture off before he—

She turned around and stared at him.

He did not think her eyes could grow wider.

Fortunately, he happened to have his trousers in his hand and covering his private parts. Not on, just held in front. "What are you doing, Fiona?"

"You sprayed me with seawater."

"Accidentally. Why are you standing so close to my clothes? I only meant to dry off a little."

"Oh, I should have thought to bring a towel for you."

"We'll think of it tomorrow."

A little pulse beat at the base of her throat. "You are going to swim tomorrow?"

He nodded. "If weather permits. Now, I don't mind standing here naked while holding a casual conversation with you, but I would like to don my clothes before nightfall."

She turned to face away from him. Still quite close.

This was a good sign, he supposed. Had he been that drunken goat, Lord Dexter, she would have shot up those stairs faster than a stone hurled from a catapult to avoid him.

She was looking at him again when he bent to retrieve his shirt. Droplets trailed down his neck, chest, and arms, so he lightly rubbed his shirt along his upper torso before slipping it over his head.

"Fiona?"

She gulped. "Forgive me for staring, but Shoreham looked nothing like you."

"I know."

"This is why every woman in England wants you," she said, her voice shaky.

"They want me because I am a duke and rich. The body itself is immaterial. So is my heart. Immaterial, that is."

"A duke," she murmured. "I wish you were a stable groom or a footman."

"You wouldn't marry me if I were either of those men."

"Then a barrister or a gentleman squire."

He nodded. "That would work."

"But you are not those things," she said with that hint of pain in her voice that always crushed him.

"No, and I never will be. I am a duke and this will not change while I am alive."

"I know."

Tears welled in her eyes.

"Stop that, Fiona," he said gently, and took her by the hand to lead her to their blanket beside the steps so they could put on their shoes and close the picnic basket.

The sun had reached its zenith and was now beginning its descent. Birds hovered over the water, hunting for fish. They still had hours yet before sunset, but Rob felt his hopes fade along with the beautiful light.

It was only the first day. They had not even spent a night

together. But he could see by the way Fiona responded to this outing, her lips trembling as though she were about to weep, that she had her mind made up already.

She was never going to marry him.

He did not know if he could ever persuade her to alter this decision, not even if they spent the next seven days in mindless carnal bliss in her bed.

But he was going to try his best. This was not merely about weakening her resistance with the use of his prowess. Intimacy was only one aspect of the marital bond he needed to create with Fiona.

Weakening her resistance with true love was his ultimate goal.

He kept hold of her hand as they climbed the steps together, and carried their belongings in the other. They crossed the small expanse of grass and entered the woodsy path that led back to the house. The wind had died down now, as it often did in the late afternoon.

When she slipped her hand from his as they approached the house, he tried to keep his hopes from dying, too.

"I'll have a bath brought up to you," she said, rushing into the house ahead of him.

He wanted to invite her to join him, but held his tongue. There would be time enough for that over the course of the week.

"What do you have planned for us after supper? Any particular entertainments?"

She surprised him by turning flustered. "Oh… I…did not think of that."

Fiona *never* got flustered.

"Well, we could play cards," she said. "Or read. Or…"

"Or what?"

"Well, nothing… *You know.*"

Yes, he did know. "Are you suggesting we go straight to your bedchamber and have at it?"

CHAPTER FOUR

S UPPER WAS A quiet affair, a simple meal of rabbit stew and a lemon syllabub for dessert, after which Fiona suggested she and Rob take a walk to the beach to watch the sunset. "Not down the steps, just to stand at the top of them and enjoy the sun disappear into the water. What do you think?"

"Sounds perfect. We had better bring a lantern for the way back."

She nodded. There was something so achingly good about being with him. Perhaps because he knew her so well and had seen her go through every stage of her life. "That's a fine idea."

He was also the perfect blend of kind and patient, ready to tease her but never coerce her into doing something she was not ready to do. This bedding thing was surprisingly disconcerting to her.

She wanted to do it.

Dear heaven.

It was *shocking* how eagerly she desired it.

But making treasured memories with him would also be incredibly painful because each shared moment also marked an approaching end.

As though sensing her thoughts, he took her hand, entwining their fingers—and with it their hearts—as they walked along the familiar path to the water.

But she was trying to untangle their hearts.

Not today. The hurt and despair would come soon enough, so why rush it?

He slipped an arm around her waist when they reached the beach steps, neither of them saying anything as they watched the sun's fading rays catch the clouds and turn them to fiery shades of red, orange, and yellow across the sky.

A blaze of twilight lingered for another few minutes. Fiona knew it would leave enough illumination for them to return to the manor house without having to bother lighting the lantern. "Let's go," she said before the ache of darkness marked the passage of another day and became too difficult to ignore.

She had a dozen memories from these past hours alone with Rob that she needed to write in her journal while they were still fresh in her mind. Not that she would ever forget a single moment of these days of heaven, but the details could be forgotten and the recollections distorted over time.

"All right," he said, sounding just as wistful, "and what's next?"

It was too early for them to retire for the night, since her staff would notice and start wondering if there was something going on between them. Perhaps it was foolish of her to care, or to believe anyone would be deceived even though their rooms were far apart. "Um, we could read or play cards, as I mentioned earlier. I would offer to play the pianoforte, but I am not very good at it. Cherish is the one who plays divinely."

He grinned. "I know. I've heard her…and I've heard you. No pianoforte."

She laughed and gave him a light smack on the arm. "Beast. That wasn't polite."

"No, but truthful. I'm not judging, since I cannot play at all. Do you mind if we just sit in the parlor and read?"

"Not at all. I have some writing to do, so I'll sit at my desk while you settle in comfortably with a book. Would you like a brandy, too?"

He nodded. "Will you join me?"

She winced. "I've never acquired a taste for it."

"A glass of wine, then?"

She usually drank tea, but wine would also serve to calm her nerves. She hadn't imbibed enough of it as they ate their stew.

When the clock chimed the eleven o'clock hour and it had fallen quite dark outside, Simmons appeared. "My lady, shall I close up the house now?"

Rob shut his book and stood up. "I'll take care of it before I retire. Is there anything I should not overlook?"

"No tricks or secrets to this house, Your Grace. Just make certain the windows and doors on this main floor are locked. I have already taken care of the kitchen and the staff area. Front door is already locked, too."

"I'll attend to the rest. Have a good evening, Simmons."

"You as well, Your Grace." He then turned to address Fiona and wish her a good evening.

"And you, Simmons," she replied, nodding to dismiss him.

With her butler now gone, Rob returned to reading his book, his manner casual, as though this was not the night he would undress her and spend it doing all sorts of shameful things with her and to her.

She thought of Shoreham and how he had always approached her.

But Rob was different. He was going to undress her, wasn't he? Was this not why he had made a show of taking off his clothes and swimming earlier today?

Well, he could have done that simply because he was hot and wanted to swim to cool himself down.

She finished writing the last of the entries in her journal and cleared her throat.

Utter silence from Rob.

She cleared her throat again.

He peered up from his book, one eyebrow arched. "Catching a cold?"

"No, I am fine. I think we ought to close up the house now."

He smiled. "Yes, m'lady. Why don't you run up to your bed-chamber while I take care of securing the windows and doors?"

She nodded and drank the last droplets of her wine, practically licking her glass clean and debating whether to pour herself another glass for courage.

Honestly, she was behaving like a goose.

And for what? She had been married for almost two decades and knew all about carnal visits. Well, Shoreham was not quite the brash, heat-of-passion sort of fellow. No, indeed. He was best described as a considerate husband.

But Rob?

Panther eyes. Powerful body. It was because of *him* she was feeling like a fluttering goose.

Were it any other man, she wouldn't care and be completely relaxed. Of course, were it any other man, she would not be considering doing what she was willing and aching to do with him.

She grabbed her journal and scurried upstairs to her bed-chamber, needing to put it under lock and key before anyone found it and read it.

The things she had written about his body, and wanting to do to his body... Utterly naughty. Lustful. Not merely crude, but banned-from-church lewd.

Now, if only she could be so brave in actuality.

She must have been lost in her thoughts longer than she realized, because she had done little more than lock away her journal, begin to unlace her gown, then change her mind and unpin her hair first, intending to brush it out.

She had not even reached for her hairbrush before Rob was suddenly standing in the doorway, arms folded across his chest as he waited for her invitation to enter. "May I?" he asked.

Had she not been inviting him all day long with her moon-eyed looks?

She nodded. "I left the door open hoping you would."

He strode in and shut it behind him.

"Let me help you," he said in a soft, melt-your-soul, seductive voice that filled her with anticipation.

She gulped.

The air between them suddenly turned incendiary because of those fiery looks he was tossing at her. All at once, she could not breathe.

Nor could he, it seemed.

"Fiona," he said in an aching whisper as he approached, stopping inches from her to stare at her with her hair down and her gown loosened so that one sleeve slipped off her shoulder. He smiled and gently ran his fingers through her curls. "Silky."

She wanted to laugh. Her locks had always been too wild for Shoreham's liking.

She shoved the wayward curls back with her fingers, and hadn't the time to reply before he kissed her lightly on the one bare shoulder and then drew her into his arms.

Was this really about to happen?

"Fiona," he repeated, crushing his mouth down on hers. She felt the white-hot press of his lips capturing hers and swallowing her up in a scorching kiss. Pure fire. Every inch of her was now singed.

There were different levels of fire—everyone knew this. Blue being the coolest flame, then red, then blinding white, like a flash of lightning that strikes in an instant and burns you to ashes.

This was his level of heat.

Oh, his mouth felt so good on hers. Crushing. Demanding. Possessive.

But also achingly tender.

Her body combusted as her bosom came into contact with the hard wall of his chest and her hip grazed his thigh. Her blood turned molten and flowed like lava through her veins.

This fiery explosion was to be expected because they had been together all afternoon and into the night, two unlit powder kegs of repressed desire. It took only one of them to set the other off.

He worked the lacings of her gown while consuming her with this first kiss, his fingers nimble despite the quivering urgency both of them were feeling.

She just wanted to rip the clothes off him.

"Slow down, Fiona." He laughed and then kissed her deeply again, as though reaching for her soul.

He moved her backward to the bed without breaking contact with her mouth. No doubt he had done this before, for he was quite smooth going about it.

She tugged at his shirt, attempting to pull it over his massive shoulders, but this caused them to stumble onto the mattress instead and awkwardly end the kiss. He had to catch himself and roll to the side before he fell atop her.

First he laughed, and then he groaned. Such an aching groan. "I wanted to take it slow with you, Fiona."

"I know. Much appreciated but completely unnecessary." She was still trying to peel his shirt of him.

"I'll do it." He gave another agonized laugh before shedding it with a quick and careless masculine movement that involved flexing muscles and straining sinews.

Oh. Dear. Heaven.

"Your gown next." He kissed her neck as his fingers worked the last of her lacings and set off little fires in her body.

Magic fingers. He always did have glorious hands.

He tossed her gown aside and settled atop her even though she still had on her chemise. He had kept his trousers on. Did he think she needed to be treated as gently as an innocent?

It was true that she was not proficient in the sexual arts and would never be a proper courtesan. But she wasn't *completely* ignorant. "Do not take it slow, Rob. I'll panic and think too much if you do."

"I was not planning to charge at you like a raging bull," he said, regarding her quite lovingly. "Are you sure, Fiona? I don't want to rush this first time between us. But the sight of you with your hair down and your gown slipping off your shoulders…

Everything is flying out of my head, and all I want to do is devour you."

"Then do so. I won't stop you."

He kissed her again, his mouth hot and persistent, while also running his hands over her body as though he needed to memorize each and every curve and hollow. She did the same with his, the recognition surprisingly profound even though she had never touched him like this before.

He rained kisses upon her lips, her chin, and then suckled the tender spot below her ear before moving lower and doing the same to her breast.

She gasped and arched beneath him as lightning bolts tore through her.

He looked up and studied her in surprise. "Dear Lord, Fiona. Is this your first time?"

That any man had touched her breast with his mouth? She was too humiliated to answer.

He eased back slightly, and then gently kissed the swell of her breast.

But she gasped again when he renewed his onslaught, closing his mouth once more over the taut bud through the thin fabric of her chemise and lightly suckling it. Ripples of pleasure tore through her, the delicious shock making her cry out.

His body tensed, his muscles coiled like that of a cobra, as he took his lips off her and looked up again.

"Don't stop." She drew his head back to her bosom. "I cried out because I liked it."

His laugh was painful. "So did I…like it, that is. Then you are all right with what I am doing?"

At her nod, he tugged her chemise lower to expose her breast, then proceeded to tease and lick the creamy mound with exquisite care, now understanding no one had ever done this to her before.

Her head was in a spin, for relations with Shoreham had been nothing like this. Never passionate or set-flames-to-the-bed hot.

Always discreet. Polite. Done.

However, with Rob, it was hearts blown wide open. Every touch of his mouth was a scorching demand for her surrender. His every kiss and smile was an ardent declaration of his love.

Well, she was going to let him declare that he loved her as often as he wished for these next seven days.

And then they would walk away from each other.

They *had* to walk away. For his sake and to save his dukedom.

"I hear you thinking," he said, his voice a soft growl, as he shifted lower down her body. She was not certain what he meant to do, but she trusted him.

It did not matter what he planned next. She was his for now and always, although she would never admit the *always* part.

"I am not thinking at all." She tugged on his hair, liking the soft, wavy feel of those dark-gold strands as she sank her fingers in them. "I cannot even recall my own name."

He nudged the hem of her chemise upward so that the garment bunched around her waist. She wasn't certain why he had tugged it down and now up, when he could have just slipped it off her and cast it aside with the other clothes now strewn on the carpet.

But there was a bit of prurient naughtiness in leaving it on and yet covering nothing.

"What are you going to do next?" she asked.

"Must I draw you a map?" His shoulders were now between her legs. *Dear heaven.* This was too, too shocking. "Do you really not know, Fiona?"

"I have my suspicions." She had read books that went into some detail. Also, some of her women friends had whispered about the sort of things they did with their lovers. But she had listened only with half an ear, for these were not happily married women.

She had never considered herself to be in their situation. Indeed, she had been content with Shoreham and grown used to his no-frolic attitude. He may not have been exciting, but he had always been considerate when performing his marital duties.

Besides, she had taken her marriage vows seriously. How could she ever betray that kind man?

Stars blazed in her eyes when Rob put his mouth to her most intimate spot and began to tease and suckle as he had done with the bud of her breast. Fiery comets sped past her and burst into flames as his tongue touched her where it had no right to be.

Rob had his hand on her stomach, gentling her as she squirmed. But how could she not wriggle about when he was exciting her to the very core?

If he did not want her to move, then he needed to get his head out from between her legs and stop licking her as though she were ice cream.

Oh, dear heaven. That sounded so dirty!

But it felt so good.

"Rob…" She called his name urgently as her entire body suddenly turned volcanic and seemed about to explode from within. *"Rob."*

"I have you, Fiona. Let yourself go."

How?

She had never experienced anything so intense, and now felt herself coming undone as quivering waves began to ripple through her body.

She cried his name again. Blinding stars filled her eyes and then tore apart to become shimmering bits of starlight. She began to tumble through this blaze of starlight, tumble toward Rob, who was there to catch her as she fell, just as he had always been and could forever be, if only she would let him.

She had never felt anything this powerful before.

But she felt safe throughout the entire experience, because this was Rob and he would always care for her.

She stayed floating through the silvery sparkles of starlight as they fell gently in a shimmering rain that now surrounded her. Her breathless journey was about to come to an end.

No mere journey, but a beautiful moment in time.

Rob took her in his arms as she calmed, his kisses soft and loving. He slid his hands up and down her arms, caressing her while she regained her composure.

She rested her head upon his bare chest, her escape of air feathering his chest hairs as she nestled against him and inhaled his clean, rugged scent of musk and maleness. His skin felt hot against her cheek.

She threw her arm across his torso, as though this was enough to hold him to her forever. But she'd never had enormous strength in her arms. She could not hold him back if he wanted to go.

And he would have to go soon.

She forced her mind back to the *now* and not the inevitable, heart-shattering future.

"How do you feel, Fiona?"

"Shamefully good. Astounded. Not quite recovered from whatever that was."

He chuckled. "It's called pleasure."

She had heard the word used so often with regard to the bedchamber, but never understood the power of it.

How could she have possibly been so dense? Why had Shoreham never tried this in all the years of their marriage?

But somehow, it felt right that Rob should be the one to show her the true meaning of pleasure. "I think I'll swim with you tomorrow, Rob."

A smile tugged at the corners of his sinfully beautiful mouth. "Good."

She sighed. "It's the clothes, you see."

"What about clothes?"

"Mine are half on, half off, and bunched around my waist," she explained. "Whether they are on or off doesn't matter. That I held back today and chose not to swim with you doesn't change the truth of things. You see right through me to my heart. Even if I wore layers upon layers of winter clothes, you would still see through them into my heart. You would even see me clearly through a wall of iron, for that matter."

"You give me too much credit. All I had was a desire to share a moment like this with you," he said, his voice low and rumbling, "and a hope that it might please you. I was going to slowly teach you the ways of desire—inching steps, although I did not think you would be afraid of anything."

"I'm not when I am with you," she admitted.

"However, I was worried that you would think too hard about what we were doing and shy away. I wanted to gain your trust."

"Trust in your mastery?"

He grinned and rolled his eyes. "But this is better. Just a raw explosion of feeling. A hot mess. Nothing planned."

She nodded. "And nothing held back."

In all her married years, she had never lain unclothed beside Shoreham.

It felt so natural with Rob. She was nestled against his bare chest, her bosom pressed against his warm skin, and all she wanted was to stay this way all night.

And tomorrow she was going to swim with him.

She did not know what this signified beyond two friends going into the water together. She had several bathing gowns—most were wool and designed for modesty by the shore, but not for actual swimming. The material was too heavy when wet and would weigh her down.

For this reason, she'd had two others made for her that were of black cotton and more practical for going into the water. She did not know how easy they were to remove when wet, but Rob was a resourceful fellow and would figure out a way, assuming they were going to do something more than take an innocent swim together.

He worked his magic on her once more that night, stealing her breath and her soul as she soared to these newly discovered heights of passion.

Starlight surrounded her again. Beautiful, glittering, and silvery.

Would this always happen with him?

Always only meant these next seven days, she reminded herself.

His gentle caresses lulled her to sleep. The next thing she knew, it was morning and the sun was shining into her bedchamber. She liked to sleep with the drapes drawn open because she enjoyed waking up to the warmth of the sun on her face.

When she turned to greet Rob, she found the other side of her bed was empty. It was as though he had never been here.

An ache tore through her heart and left a gaping hole in it.

She glanced down at herself. Her chemise was back in proper order, which meant he must have adjusted it sometime during the night. She hadn't felt a thing, no doubt because she had been thoroughly satiated and fallen into a deep, restful slumber.

The gown she'd worn yesterday was neatly folded and placed atop the back of a chair. It was as though all traces of him had been removed from her room.

Except she still felt him on her skin, his warm lips and that devil of a tongue having branded her as his.

She also caught the musky scent of him on her sheets. It was only the slightest trace, but this was still dangerous. A servant with a sensitive nose would smell it and know. Since she did not want any gossip going around, she scampered out of bed and grabbed a bottle of her favorite perfume. *Desire* was what they called the fragrance, and she now sprinkled several droplets onto his side of the bed. "There, good as new."

She tossed on a robe and went to her balcony to peer out.

The sun was rising above the horizon and shedding its light all around, but a morning mist still lingered at the edges of the trees. Because of the mist, Fiona knew it was still early. Probably not quite seven o'clock in the morning, by her guess.

To her surprise, Rob was not only awake, but he appeared to have taken a morning ride. He was dressed casually, just a plain work shirt and buff riding breeches as he strode back toward the house.

He looked up, saw her, and smiled.

She waved. "I'll meet you downstairs. Have you had your breakfast yet?"

"No, I was waiting for you."

"I'll be down in fifteen minutes." She rang for her maid to assist with her gown, but did not wait for her to appear before tossing water into her basin to wash herself. She then grabbed her hairbrush.

She had just finished brushing her hair when there came a soft knock at her door that she recognized as that of her lady's maid, Molly. "Come in," she called out, bustling to her armoire to decide what to wear this morning. Her swim with Rob would not take place until this afternoon because the seawater did not properly heat up until the sun had beaten down on it for hours. "Oh, Molly. I need your help. What shall I wear?"

Her maid smiled. "The duke is quite the handsome devil, isn't he? Here, you ought to wear this pale blue with the flowers embroidered on it. You will steal his breath away."

"All right. But I am not interested in the Duke of Durham in that way."

Molly arched an eyebrow. "Sure, I believe that. Then why are you fluttering like a crazed butterfly this morning?"

"Nonsense." Fiona blushed. "I am too old to be fluttering, and I am certainly not crazed."

"Then what is it that has you in a dither? Flux? Loose bowels? Indigestion?"

"Molly!" She shook her head and laughed softly.

"Every woman alive is going to swoon whenever that man is around. And you are not too old to count yourself out, m'lady. He certainly does not think so. We've all seen the way he looks at you. I'm surprised this house has not burned to ashes with those fiery glances he casts your way whenever he thinks no one is looking. But I won't say another word because I know what you are thinking and feeling."

She gave Fiona a hug, knowing she could do this because Molly had been a savior to her after Shoreham had died. "Grab your moment of happiness, m'lady. Do not care what anyone else may think. You are a lady through and through. Nothing you do will change this."

Fiona had Molly next help her fashion her hair in a simple bun at the nape of her neck. Her hair was softly pulled back except for a few curls that fell over her brow and framed her face. "All done, m'lady."

"Thank you, Molly." She cast her a warm smile before hurrying downstairs.

Rob was standing in the parlor, staring out one of the large windows, when she walked into the room. He turned, smiled, and gave a low whistle. "You're looking lovely this morning."

She laughed. "So are you."

He *did* look magnificently handsome.

She could not suppress the blush that now stained her cheeks at the recollection of his big, muscled body atop hers last night, and the things he did to her with his magical touch. The man understood a woman's body, this was for certain. He especially understood hers, but this was because of the deep connection of their hearts.

Perhaps this was the reason he had made her feel cherished. The entire night was an expression of his abiding love.

"It looks nice outside," she said. "Shall we have our breakfast on the terrace?"

"Sure."

Since the salvers were already set out atop the dining room buffet, they served themselves there and then carried the food out to one of the outdoor tea tables.

Fiona did not know whether it was his company that made her eggs and sausages taste better than ever, or whether she was just famished after last night's exertions. She had soared amid starlight *twice* last night.

By the way he looked at her this morning, she knew he meant to make that a dozen times more before the week was through.

Perhaps she ought to stop thinking of him as a Silver Duke—he was too young to be admitted into their ranks, even though the *ton* had now dubbed him as one because of the dash of silver threaded through his dark-gold hair.

He could be her Starlight Duke.

Yes, that was better.

"What's our plan today, Fiona?" he asked before taking a sip of his coffee. "Other than swimming later."

"Well, we could play lawn games. Take a long walk in the countryside. Take horses and ride."

He shook his head to dismiss all the suggestions, which surprised her, because he rarely voiced a preference when it came to house party activities, and usually just went along. Well, this was no true house party, not with him as her only guest.

Still, was it not the same sort of thing?

"Then what do you want to do, Rob? Any better ideas?"

"Let me take you to Brighton. We can walk around and do a little shopping. Perhaps find a pretty spot overlooking the water and grab a bite to eat. Then return here for a late afternoon swim."

She smiled at him. "Actually, that sounds wonderful."

"Good. Grab your things and let's go."

She polished off the last of her breakfast and ran upstairs to collect her gloves, stylish hat, and reticule, as well as a light wrap on the chance the weather turned cooler. But the mist off the water had already melted away, a sign this was to be another hot, dry summer day.

Once ready, Molly accompanied her downstairs. They both had the same heart-stopping reaction to the sight of Rob leaning against the open doorway, his arms folded across his chest and the sun shining its golden aura upon his hair while he conversed with Simmons. The summer sun had lightened his hair in perfect shadings of wheat amid the dark gold.

As a little boy, his hair had been that lighter hue but was now naturally darkened with maturity. He still looked glorious, especially with that added trace of silver at his temples.

Just a dash.

Hardly noticeable.

But devastating in effect.

"Oh, Molly. It isn't fair, is it?"

"No, m'lady," the maid said with a whispered chuckle. "I'm happily married and still would leap into bed with that man if he crooked his finger and bade me forward. But it isn't me or any other woman he wants. His eyes always devour you."

Because he had panther eyes.

He turned for the briefest moment and cast Fiona that devouring look.

"We'll be back in the afternoon," she said, placing a hand over her stomach as her butterflies began to flutter. "Oh, I should take a moment to ask Mrs. Harris if we need anything from Brighton."

Her housekeeper insisted that they needed nothing and shooed her off. "Do not think of anything but that impossibly handsome man."

Even staid, proper Mrs. Harris?

Fiona sighed and joined Rob as he stood beside the carriage. "Did your housekeeper assign us any chores?"

"No, not a one," she said as he helped her into his impressive ducal conveyance with its embossed lions on the crest.

He settled in the seat across from hers. "Good. Then all we have to think about is us."

She felt a twinge in her heart and then a rougher twist. However, she forced a smile to hide her ache.

There would never be an *us*.

But there could be the pretense of it, just for today.

They made idle conversation on the ride to Brighton, their manner casual and friendly, Fiona pretending not to feel the heat and raw craving that thickened the air between them. And what of last night? Could she overlook the ravenous passion between them as they clawed each other in desperation?

She regretted not bringing a fan, for the memory of her wanton behavior was hard to ignore, and she needed cooling off.

Had he noticed her embarrassment? What did he think of last night? Rob was very good at masking his feelings.

She was not.

He sighed. "Fiona, do you want to talk about it? Us. What we did."

She shook her head vehemently. "No."

His grin was affectionate as he said, "All right."

There was an extended silence between them before she groaned and asked, "How was it for you? I mean…how was I? I'm sure you've done this with other ladies. But…"

"I was with *you*, Fiona." He leaned forward to place his hand gently over hers. "How else would it be but the best experience of my life?"

She cast him a wry smile. "Good answer."

He chuckled.

She wanted to ask more questions, but held back. Rob was always going to give her polite answers. Even if she had not been all that good last night, he would never say so. He would never even think so because he loved her.

Loving her first as childhood friends. Then as mature, adult friends.

And now…this.

Apparently, he adored the full package of who she was. Outspoken. Brash. Definitely stubborn. But also willing to give her full heart to him if ever he needed it or needed her.

Yes, she would give him everything she had to give…except for her hand in marriage.

The sun was blazing down on them by the time they reached the Brighton shore. Rob hopped down from the carriage and took her by the waist to help her out. "Hot as blazes already," he muttered, shading his eyes as he looked skyward.

"It was quite warm in the carriage, too," Fiona remarked. "Why don't we stop and have ices first? Then we won't feel so wilted as we walk around."

He cast her a wicked smile. "Ices?"

"Yes, aren't you in need of cooling down?"

He nodded. "Yes, every time I look at you."

"Oh, good grief. Behave yourself."

"Not a chance." He led her toward one of the confectionery shops, the grin still on his lips.

She paused to stare up at him. "All right, I give up. What is so wickedly funny about our having ices?"

"Must I spell it out for you?"

"Yes." She cast him an impatient glance. This was another one of her failings—impatience.

But he seemed to take it all in stride. "It isn't about the ices, it is that we must lick them to eat them. Get it? Lick. L-I-C-K."

"Ugh! Rob!"

"Do not berate me because I like *your* flavor, Fiona."

She covered her eyes, although this would do nothing to keep her from hearing what else he had to say.

He laughed softly and drew her hands off her face. "What remains to be answered is…"

"What? Stop grinning and just tell me."

"Whether you are going to like the flavor of *me*."

"What?" Her eyes widened and her mouth gaped open. "I don't know how to respond to that. Do ladies do this to…"

"Men? And their private parts?"

She nodded. "People do that? Is this what I…?"

He tucked a finger under her chin, nudging it upward to close her mouth.

He studied her for a long moment and frowned. "Here's the deal. We do *nothing* unless you are willing. Your answer will not change my feelings toward you. This is completely up to you."

"Should I not consider what you might like?"

A smile quirked the corners of his mouth. "It would be appreciated. But again, not necessary."

She contemplated the matter as they sat overlooking the water, a salty breeze swirling around them as they ate their ices.

She tried not to watch him as he put his mouth to the shavings, swirled his tongue over them, and licked the drippings with his tongue.

How *would* he taste? The notion was appalling.

Did she dare?

CHAPTER FIVE

ROB HAD NOT realized quite the extent to which Shoreham had ignored Fiona in the bedroom. Some of what he was thinking to do with her was now stowed away in his mind and categorized as "never going to happen" or "still hope it might happen but won't hold my breath" or "yes, happening this very night."

He finished his ice shavings and watched Fiona while she was lost in her thoughts, her sweet tongue slowly licking across the last of her ice shavings. After a moment, he turned away and fixed his attention on the elegantly dressed family at the table next to them. They were not titled—this he could tell because they had their children with them and no nanny to attend them. The man was likely a barrister or wealthy merchant.

He smiled at the children, who were extremely well behaved. Polite children were something completely foreign to the aristocratic crowd in which he was raised. Parents rarely attended to their offspring, leaving the chore of raising them to be arrogant, spoiled, and pompous to their hired nannies and tutors.

Fiona had never developed any of those insufferable traits, not even after she had married Shoreham and become his countess.

As a child, she was kind and mothering. She could also be bossy, competitive, and watch out if anyone crossed her or any of her friends, because you did not want the wrath of Fiona to fall upon you.

But she was also fun, clever, and exceptionally compassionate. He had never felt so loved as when he was around her.

There was not a moment he ever regretted being with her. She always looked out for him, and yet was also ready to tell him the truth whenever he behaved like an ass. This was what made their situation so hard for him. He was no longer a little boy. It was his turn to look out for her, to protect her and make her happy.

He would walk through the fires of hell to give Fiona her heart's desire…children.

Truly, fate was cruel to them. He needed a legitimate heir to carry on the Durham title. This was the one thing she could not provide, or so she thought. What if Shoreham had been the problem all along and not her? Was this possibility not worth pursuing? Fiona seemed convinced the problem fell completely on her shoulders.

Had something happened to make her certain? Perhaps Shoreham had sired a child out of wedlock.

The notion seemed far-fetched, however. Theirs had been a marriage built on kindness and respect. While other gentlemen might have taken on mistresses or had liaisons outside of marriage, Shoreham never would have committed this utter betrayal.

Or would he?

Rob dared not raise the matter with Fiona, although he did not rule out discussing it later.

Well, he would give it thought. The topic was so sensitive for her, utterly destroying her every time it came up.

"Are you finished, Fiona?"

Her lips and tongue were ruby red from the ice syrup. "All done."

His had been a lemon ice, which perhaps had left his lips and tongue yellow. Well, they would both look ridiculous as they strolled along the shops. He asked for a cup of boiled water from a passing maid. "At once, Your Grace."

Fiona tipped her head in question. "I thought we were done. What do you want with the water?"

"To clear our mouths. We shall look like clowns otherwise."

"Oh, that would be fun." She burst into merry laughter. "We should paint bright red spots on our cheeks and noses, too, and then walk into the fanciest establishments. Do you think anyone will pass a remark when they learn you are the Duke of Durham and I am Countess Shoreham?"

She would look beautiful even with bright red spots painted all over her face. This was because Fiona was naturally pretty and nothing she did could make her look less than spectacular.

"Do not get ideas, Fiona. I am not going to walk around Brighton looking like a victim of the pox."

"Ugh, Rob! We are talking clowns, not diseases."

"Answer is still no." Once it was delivered, he waited a minute for the water to cool down, then dipped his handkerchief into the cup. After wringing it out, he dabbed the moist cloth across Fiona's supple mouth to wipe off the red syrup, and then did the same with his to wipe away the yellow.

She cast him an impish smile. "Your tongue is still yellow, Rob."

"I'll try not to stick it out. Yours is still red. Do not talk or stick yours out, either."

"I always talk."

He grinned. "I know, but try to keep your mouth pinched tightly closed, then no one will be the wiser. Or...I could kiss you inappropriately and we'd both have orange tongues. You know, mix yellow and red, get orange."

She tossed an ice shaving at him. "Keep your yellow tongue to yourself, Your Grace."

He angled left and the ice shaving missed him and fell to the floor, quickly melting under the heat of the day. "You never could aim straight. Come on. Let's go before we start an ice fight in here. Where to next?"

"Would you mind if we browsed the shops?"

"Not at all. Hurrah, sounds like oodles of fun."

"Do not be sarcastic," she said with a trill of laughter. "Were you not the one who suggested this outing? I would have been content beating you with a croquet mallet."

"Oof, violence does not become you."

"I meant beating you in a game, not actually hitting you over the head until your brains spilled out."

"Delightful." He rose and offered his arm. "Besides, as I said, your aim is execrable. You could never beat me at any lawn games that require an accurate eye and a steady hand."

She tipped her chin up in playful defiance. "Challenge is on, Durham. I shall have you weeping because I am going to beat you so badly, you shall be on your knees in utter devastation."

"Oh, you think so? A complete rout? That will never happen, demon who has taken possession of Fiona's body." He led her out of the confectionery shop, his chuckle light and playful as he held open the door for her. "But let's wait for Cherish's house party guests to arrive before we play for points. I want to have an audience when I soundly defeat you."

She laughed as they started down the street toward the elegant shops. "You are such a fake, Rob. All I'd have to do is sniffle and pretend I am about to cry, and your soft heart would melt and let me win."

"Consider me warned." He paused to peer in the window of a jeweler's shop. "Come inside with me. Lots of sparkly things to catch your eye."

"Ooh, pretty. You should buy a trinket for the young lady you choose to marry."

"You know our deal," he said more sternly than intended, but the mention of anyone other than her occupying his heart just made him bitter. "I don't offer for anyone until three months has passed."

"Fine," she said, turning away a moment so he would not see the flash of pain in her eyes. But she hadn't turned away fast enough, and he saw her smile crumble. "Why must you be so stubborn? You know the wait is unnecessary. Nothing is going to happen with me. Did you notice those children at the table next to ours?"

He nodded, giving her cheek a light caress. "I did."

"Weren't they lovely?" She cast him a fragile smile, obviously forcing herself to ignore her own pain and be happy for this family who were living *her* dream. "I wanted to reach out and hug them," she said, her voice shaky. "A boy and a girl. How sweet they were. That's what you must have for yourself."

He put a finger to her lips. "Not thinking about it for the rest of this week, and nor should you. Come on, you're my hostess. It is right that I choose a gift for you. Tell me what you like."

"It isn't necessary."

"I know. I still want to get you something nice." He put his arm around her to offer comfort for the terrible ache he knew she was feeling. "Diamonds? Rubies? Sapphires? Emeralds? Anything catch your eye?"

He could easily afford to buy her every beautiful piece in the shop. However, he knew it wasn't the gems Fiona wanted. Pretty sparkles did not interest her. She wanted something that held meaning for both of them.

She said no to the diamonds and sapphires the jeweler brought out to show her. Refused the glittering necklaces, bracelets, brooches, and earrings on display. "They sparkle like the stars," the jeweler said, hoping to coax Fiona into selecting something expensive. "Don't you love starlight, m'lady?"

"I do," Fiona said, giving Rob an impish smile.

But she remained firm in her resolve, for she was all about sentiment.

"Would you happen to have a brooch of a clown eating an orange ice?" Rob asked, grinning at Fiona.

The jeweler looked at him cross-eyed. "No, Your Grace. Surely you jest."

"Oh, no. He is absolutely serious," Fiona replied, unable to resist a chuckle.

His absurd comment had put a genuine gleam of joy on her face.

Her beautiful face.

"Or a cameo brooch of a lady holding a croquet mallet upraised in her hand?" Rob added, making a show of holding a mallet and swinging it into the air as though about to bring it crashing down on someone's head.

The poor jeweler looked perplexed.

Fiona took pity on him. "A cameo brooch might be just the thing, but depicting a more classical design. The Muses, perhaps."

"I have something better." His eyes brightened suddenly. "I just received a shipment of rings and amulets made by Italian artisans. The stones themselves are of lapis lazuli, a blue healing stone brought to the ancient land of Egypt from one of the mountainous regions along the Silk Road. These stones signify wisdom and truth. They are also considered to be love stones."

Rob nodded. The fellow had caught on.

The jeweler rushed through a curtain into his back room and returned with a large box. Opening it, he began to set out several of the blue pieces on a cloth of softest white velvet. "This amulet is a depiction of Isis, goddess of love and fertility. See how the blue glistens. There is no deeper, richer blue than lapis lazuli."

Fiona tensed almost imperceptibly.

Rob felt her response at the mention of fertility because he had his hand lightly resting on the small of her back.

"And this ring?" Rob asked, pointing to a rounded stone in a plain setting.

"Also lapis lazuli, Your Grace. Magical, don't you think? The wearer shall know wisdom and truth."

Fiona was staring at it in utter fascination.

"I'll take the ring. And the amulet. Can you have the amulet set in a necklace?"

The jeweler eagerly nodded. "Yes, it is already fitted with a clasp to be put on a gold chain. Suitable for a bracelet or a necklace."

"Good. Show us some gold chains," Rob said.

After selecting several necklace chains for Fiona, Rob made arrangements to pay the jeweler.

Fiona walked out of the shop while he finished his transactions, but Rob took her absence as an opportunity to add one more item to his purchases. A healing stone, just the chunk of it that was thick and not yet formed into any piece of jewelry. Was it possible there was a magical aspect to these stones? He would willingly dance naked around a bonfire with antlers on his head if that were needed to unleash its mystical strength.

Yes, he would do anything if there were a chance these talismans could work to heal Fiona. After all, miracles were known to occur. Not that he believed in them, for he was quite cynical about life and its rewards. In truth, he had lost faith years ago.

Still, unexplained things occasionally happened.

He glanced up at the firmament. "Prove me wrong…please."

He would give Fiona the ring and amulet after supper tonight, but would keep the rock for himself until he figured out the perfect spot to place it in her home.

For now, he would tuck it in one of the bureau drawers in his guest chamber, the drawer where he kept his undergarments. No one was going to dig through there, and it was no one's business what he planned to do with that stone.

"Stupid clot," he muttered to himself, knowing he would have laughed at anyone else doing the same.

If Fiona rejected his offering of that chunk of stone, then he would keep it and be the proud owner of a pretty paperweight to hold down his documents while he worked in his study with the windows open.

It was after six o'clock by the time they returned to Shoreham Manor, both of them hot, tired, and ready for a quick swim. Fiona's maid helped her change out of her gown and into a bathing gown. But Rob had to wait to see her in it, for Fiona came down the stairs wearing a billowing bathing robe that covered her from shoulder to foot.

Too bad. The blasted thing was too big for her slight body and looked hideous.

"Here," Mrs. Harris said, scrambling toward her with a large pouch as she marched downstairs. "Towels and a blanket for you and His Grace."

Rob took it out of her hands. "I have it."

"Oh, perfect. Thank you for thinking of us," Fiona said, smiling at her housekeeper.

Rob struggled to suppress a grin, watching Fiona as she placed a bathing hat on her head. It was more of a mobcap than a stylish hat, but had the same effect of making her eyes look enormous. Sparkling and beautiful.

Gad, she looked adorable.

Of course, she would look even more fetching with that monstrosity of a robe off her.

Rob had stripped down to an old shirt and work trousers. "Ready?"

She looked up at him and cast him a melting smile. "Yes. Let's go."

They made their way down to the beach.

He grinned with appreciation when Fiona took off her robe to reveal the bathing costume. It was of black cotton instead of the usual wool that was impossible to wear if one wished to swim, for the wool absorbed water and would sink a swimmer. Her very practical cotton outfit came down only as far as her knees, revealing an expanse of shapely leg. The matching black cap had little white ribbons on it similar to those on her bathing gown.

Rob soaked her in along with the sunshine. Fiona had the sort of face that looked great in hats, caps, bonnets, anything placed atop her head. They made her eyes look bigger. Like aquamarine pools to drown in.

She had a body men would fight wars over, too. The allure of Helen of Troy came to mind.

He tugged off his shirt and boots but decided to swim wearing his trousers.

He wasn't sure why. Perhaps he wasn't up to pushing Fiona beyond her limits just now. She had seen him naked last night, but he did not feel it was appropriate to fully reveal himself again this afternoon.

No particular reason for this bit of modesty, just a prickle up his neck. And he never ignored those prickles.

Just why he had them was not clear to him yet, but they had him on alert.

"Come in with me, Rob. It's a beautiful day and the water is quite calm. I'll race you to the rocks and back." She pointed to an outcropping at the edge of their sheltered cove. It served as a boundary for swimmers, because going beyond it meant one had to deal with the swifter currents of the English Channel, and few people were strong enough to battle those.

"You know I am going to win, Fiona. I'm the stronger swimmer. How about we just swim lazily along the length of the beach? I do not like the idea of us getting so close to that open water."

She sighed. "All right. I never knew you to be so cautious. Those rocks aren't very far and we would not go beyond them. Oh, and look. My neighbor's sons are rowing out to that outcropping now. See, over there."

Rob frowned. The boys looked to be young, no more than ten years old, and undisciplined if one judged by the way one boy was scampering about the tiny boat instead of keeping to his seat. But who could tell for certain what they intended at this distance?

Perhaps this was what his sudden unease was about. Although children were often spry on their feet, they did not understand tides or currents or quite how slippery those rocks could be.

The tide was rolling in and waves splashed with greater force against their boat, sometimes dangerously rocking it, even though those waves were mostly gentle. "Who are they? And why is there not an adult with them?" Rob asked.

"They are the Marquess of Milbury's sons, I think. The marquess purchased the neighboring property to mine last year but only moved in a few weeks ago."

He nodded. Cherish and Gawain's estate was to the west of Shoreham Manor, and now Fiona had this new neighbor to her east.

"I met him when we were in London last month," she continued. "He's a widower. I'm not sure who is taking care of his sons."

A widower? Rob did not like the sound of that.

He stared at the boys. "Obviously, no one is taking care of them at the moment."

Fiona had several rowboats of her own that she rarely used except when having one of her house parties. They were kept in a shed beside the beach steps during the summer. Rob hurried over to the shed and dragged one out.

Fiona frowned as she watched him pull it across the sand toward the water. "What are you doing?"

"What does it look like I'm doing?" He set it in the water and locked the oars in place. "I have a bad feeling about those boys. They think they are off on an adventure, and I am concerned it is about to turn tragic."

"Really, Rob? Oh, I see your point. Those rocks can be slick and treacherous. Do you think they are going to climb onto them?" she asked, following him into the water.

"Possibly."

He was about to shove his boat off toward them, but Fiona stopped him and climbed in. "I'm coming with you. You'll need my help."

"No, I can handle it. Get out, Fiona. I don't need you drowning, too."

She tipped her chin up and refused to budge. "I may not be as powerful a swimmer as you, but I am an able one. You'll need my help. Then it's settled. I'm coming with you."

Since she was now giving him a stubborn look that warned he could not move her short of setting off explosives and blasting the boat to splinters, he sighed and started rowing without further protest.

It was true, Fiona was a decent swimmer. He would not call her a strong swimmer because of her lack of upper body strength. But this had never deterred her in any of their adventures when younger.

It was also possible he *would* require her assistance, because the boys had now reached the rocks and were carelessly scampering upon them with the agile spring of little mountain goats. "Blessed saints, are they going to jump off the rocks into the water?"

Fiona's expression turned anxious. "Row faster, Rob. Oh, no. Their own boat is slipping back into the water and they haven't noticed."

"They failed to secure it properly," he muttered.

Fiona groaned. "And now the oars have dislodged and are floating away."

He doubled his speed, for the boat was now spinning in quick circles and buffeted by waves and the strengthening current. "Bloody hell. They're going to drown if they jump in at that spot."

"Why is their boat spinning so wildly?"

"There must be an undercurrent. I've seen it before—water's calm on the surface, but what lies beneath is a dangerous undertow that will drag you down and hold you in its relentless grip. Meanwhile, above it, the waters remain calm and still."

Fiona began to yell at the boys. "Stop! Danger! Sit down and don't move!"

But the boys merely waved back and climbed higher onto the rocks, unable to understand what she was calling out because the wind, despite being light and gentle, carried her voice toward the shore and not to them.

"Sit still, Fiona." Rob did not want her toppling into the water if a wave hit them while he rowed faster.

The sun glistened on the water, its rays shimmering all around them, but he was too worried to pay attention to nature's beauty right now.

They were not far from the boys when one of them suddenly lost his footing and fell with a shriek backward into the water. Rob's heart shot into his throat, for those swirling waters would spin the lad under and hold him down.

"Stay close. I might need your help." Rob shoved the oars into Fiona's hands and dove in after the boy before Fiona could do the same. Between her compassion and her competitive streak, he knew it was a distinct possibility that she'd intended to dive in first. Which also meant she would drown along with the boy, because she hadn't the muscles needed to fight a strong current.

But she wouldn't dive in now that he had gone in, for she also had enough sense to understand they could not both risk their lives, or they would help no one.

Rob felt the strong tug of the tide as he swam beneath the surface to look for the boy. The waves roiled the clear water, stirring up the bottom sand. But as he drew closer to the rocks, he saw the boy struggling and noticed blood flowing from his leg.

Doubly dangerous, for the blood would attract predators.

He grabbed the boy and shoved him upward so that his head broke through the water, and Rob soon followed.

"Grab him, Fiona," he said between great gulps of air, his voice raspy because his lungs were burning.

She had rowed closer and now tucked the oars in so that her hands were free to take hold of the boy. Rob pushed him up into the boat and then swam to the outcropping to get the younger lad, who looked to be about eight years old. He was seated on one of the flatter rocks, afraid to move and crying. "Is my brother all right?"

Rob put a comforting arm around his shoulder. "Yes, but I think he must have cut his leg on one of those sharp rocks when falling in. We'll get him tended and then deliver you home. Is your father there?"

The boy nodded. "Papa's going to kill us. We've lost the boat."

Rob glanced at their craft, which was now bobbing out to sea. "He'll get over it. A boat is replaceable but his sons are not. Who was watching you? Why were you out in the cove on your own?"

The boy cast Rob a sheepish look. "Our governess refused to leave London, so...no one is tending to us at present. Well, our Papa is, but I don't think he counts. Anyway, Papa has a meeting with several important people, so he told us to keep out of his way for an hour."

Rob arched an eyebrow. "Did he also happen to tell you to keep out of trouble?"

The boy blushed. "Yes. He might have said that, too."

"Come on, hop into our boat. We'll get your brother's leg treated and then it shall be time to face your father. I'll have Lady Shoreham send a footman over to let him know you are both safe."

"Is she Lady Shoreham?" The lad pointed to Fiona, who had taken off her bathing cap and was now pressing it to the elder boy's leg to stem the bleeding. Several of her curls had blown loose and her hair had a marvelously wild look to it. "She's beautiful."

Gad, they started young.

Or was Rob just getting old himself?

He could not help but smile as he glanced at Fiona. "Yes, she certainly is."

However, he could not think of her right now, not when getting the boys safely back on solid ground was the priority.

The boat had drawn close enough to the rocks that Rob could grab it and hold it steady while the younger lad climbed in. Then Rob did the same, trying his hardest not to capsize their tiny vessel because it was not meant to hold four people.

The water became much calmer once he rowed them away

from the rocks. With strong, swift strokes, he soon had them almost to the shore. Fiona instructed the younger boy to keep her cap firmly pressed to his brother's leg, and then hopped into the water to help Rob drag the boat onto the sand.

"That was a close call," she whispered.

He nodded. "Too close."

"You have good instincts. I would not have realized the danger until it was too late. You saved that boy's life. I'm so proud of you," she said, staring up at him with her big, gorgeous eyes.

That look.

She knew just how to make him feel like a king.

He was exhausted, but that did not stop him from casting her a wicked grin. "Does that earn me a reward?"

She laughed. "From me?"

"Well, I'd hardly ask anyone else for the reward I have in mind."

She gasped and then giggled. "Shush! The boys will hear you."

Rob did not think the pair were listening in, for they were too busy holding back tears and commiserating with each other over the punishment they felt certain to receive from their father. "I'll take the blame," the elder boy said. "I'll let him know that I forced you to go along with my idea."

"No, it was my fault. I'll tell Papa that you got hurt trying to keep me safe."

Rob noticed neither of the boys expressed any particular fear of a beating, so he expected the now-widowed marquess was not one to use physical force on his boys.

He hoped he was right. His own father had not been a kind man, usually cold, distant, and disapproving, but also one who enjoyed using his fists because he thought it would instill strength in Rob.

Utter rot. It only instilled pain, rebelliousness, and distance.

"What are your names?" he asked the pair.

"I am Lord Hatcher," the elder one said, tipping his chin up and sounding quite authoritative.

Rob grinned, for the boy was obviously proud of his courtesy title. "And your given name?"

"Oh, Jordan. Jordan Milbury. My mother's family name was Jordan, so my parents used it as my given name. This is my brother, Robert Milbury."

"Robert? That is my given name, too," Rob said, smiling at the scrawny lad.

The boy's eyes brightened. "I am a Right Honorable."

Rob's grin broadened. "I happen to be a duke. The Duke of Durham, to be precise."

Jordan laughed. "Then you outrank my father. That is a stroke of luck. Will you order him not to punish us?"

"Because we really were doing our best to behave," young Robert insisted, his eyes big and round, his expression one of utter sincerity.

Rob smothered the urge to laugh heartily at the boy's remark. Only a child would define "behaving" as rowing into dangerous currents and then climbing onto slippery, jagged rocks.

Fiona could not resist a chuckle. Her laughter spilled forth as light and gentle as a summer breeze. "Not certain how hard you were trying," she remarked. "Can you both swim?"

"Not all that well," Jordan admitted, turning to Rob. "The current was swifter than I realized. I think it would have kept me under had you not come to my rescue."

"How old are you?" Fiona asked.

"Eleven, and Rob is eight."

"Rob?" she repeated softly, and then turned to the youngster. "Is this what your friends and family call you?"

He nodded.

"This is what the duke's friends call him, too."

Both boys smiled at Rob. He felt his heart turn soft. This was why Fiona was so adamant about his marrying and siring sons. It was not so much about the title, although that was important—it was more about becoming a father and having the joys and tribulations of raising his own children.

He had felt it when first seeing those children in Brighton eating their ices, and now saving these two lads. But this only added to his turmoil, for he could not imagine anyone other than Fiona as the mother of his children.

A deep and hollow ache filled his heart.

The ache was for her. This was what she had been desperately wishing for during her marriage to Shoreham, a wish never fulfilled.

But this also gave him a sliver of worry, for the marquess was a widower and had his two sons. They appeared to be good boys, even though they had done a foolish thing. But was this not the nature of boys? To be curious and want to explore?

It was in the nature of some girls, too.

Fiona, for example. She was always taking him on adventures whenever they were together in their younger days. Hiking, climbing trees. Pretending they were pirates exploring caves to hide their booty, mostly small caves hidden among the rolling hills on either of their family estates.

Would she be so foolish as to undertake another adventure…this time without him? Would she set her cap for the marquess?

He knew the workings of her mind. By marrying the marquess and helping him raise his sons, she would not only gain a family, but make herself unavailable to *him*.

She would do this knowing he would never marry anyone else while she remained unattached.

No, Fiona.

Don't.

Nothing ever affected him, for he had faced death and misery many times before, and had endured.

But losing Fiona to another? He could not allow this to happen again. It would destroy him.

He watched her as she chatted with the boys and they looked up at her as though she were *their* fairy princess.

He suddenly felt apishly possessive.

She is my *fairy princess.*

Would the Marquess of Milbury steal her away from him?

CHAPTER SIX

ROB CARRIED JORDAN over his shoulder while he climbed the beach stairs as they returned to Shoreham Manor. Fiona held on to the younger lad's hand, keeping up a pleasant conversation to distract the child while his brother's leg continued to bleed.

Mrs. Harris came running out when she saw them approach the house. "Your Grace! What happened?"

"We caught ourselves a big fish," Rob said in light jest, although his expression remained one of worry.

Fiona quickly explained. Mrs. Harris listened as she relayed a shortened version of their adventure. "But young Lord Hatcher's leg is still bleeding. We must attend to it at once."

Her housekeeper's eyes widened. "Oh, I see. The poor lad has a nasty gash. Do you think it will require stitches? Shall I summon the doctor?"

She posed the question to Rob, but he shook his head. "I can handle it. The cut is not deep enough to require stitches, fortunately. Just bring me whiskey, boiled water, clean cloths, and bandages. And can you find something for the boys to wear? They'll need to change out of their wet clothes."

At this same moment, he realized his shirt was still on the beach along with his boots, the blanket, towels, and Fiona's belongings.

Not that he cared for Fiona's bilious robe. He hoped it would blow away on a strong gust of wind.

But his shirt was the urgent problem. He did not have one on, and this would cause a scandal for Fiona if he continued to walk around like a bare-chested ape.

He heard giggles coming from one of the upper-story bed-chambers and realized Fiona's maids were peeking at him in his shirtless splendor. They would not have behaved so giddily had they noticed the injured boy's bleeding leg. But they had fixed their gazes on him and appeared to be enjoying the show he was putting on.

Inadvertent on his part, of course.

"Mrs. Harris, I'll need a shirt for myself, too. You'll find several in the wardrobe in my chamber."

"At once, Your Grace." The housekeeper hurried off to fetch the requested items and called for a footman to retrieve their belongings from the beach.

As they waited, Rob realized Fiona was very wet and still wearing that clinging bathing gown. She had gotten a mild soaking while helping him get the boys into their boat, and then she had hopped into the water as they neared the shore, thinking to help push the boat up onto the sand.

The boys must have noticed the wetness of her outfit and been gawking at her ever since they began their walk back to the house. He ought to have realized what their impish grins signified.

"Look at me, lads," he said with a low growl, putting himself between Fiona and those curious boys who appeared to be halfway in love with her already.

They were definitely in lust with her. Fortunately, at their young ages, lust was merely a matter of intense curiosity rather than actual manly urges.

But their father was no child. How would *he* respond to Fiona?

Rob received his answer about an hour later when the Marquess of Milbury's carriage rolled up to Fiona's front door and the marquess practically tumbled out in his haste to see his boys. Fiona had, thankfully, changed into more appropriate attire and was now wearing a peach silk dinner gown that enhanced the soft beauty of her face.

She had brushed out her hair and Molly had fashioned it in a simple bun at the nape of her neck, but that drew Rob's eye to her slender neck and made him want to spend the evening kissing it and nibbling it instead of bothering with supper.

Rob had also taken a moment to change into appropriate attire. However, even though he was properly dressed, the maids still giggled and gawked at him whenever he passed by them.

If this nonsense did not die down in a day or two, he would have Fiona's housekeeper give them a stern warning. After all, this was the home of a countess and not a bawdy house, although what he and Fiona had done last night was fairly bawdy.

But that was no one's business.

He and Fiona were seated with the boys enjoying lemonade and cakes on the terrace when their father was announced. The boys looked ridiculous, for they were barefoot and now wearing some of Shoreham's old clothes that were too big for their skinny frames, even though the earl had been fairly slender himself.

Their father, a distinguished-looking gentleman of about five and forty years, took one look at his sons and sighed. "Aren't you a pair? A moment to make any father proud," he muttered, striking a note of humor amid his resignation and embarrassment.

"Papa!" They ran and hugged their father, no doubt a preemptive action to distract him from threatening them with punishment.

Rob's stomach began to churn.

Was Fiona considering Milbury?

In truth, the man would even fit in as a Silver Duke. That he was merely a marquess was irrelevant. He was rich, titled, a widower, and had a dash of silver at his temples that many women seemed to find irresistible.

Would Bromleigh, Lynton, and Camborne soon open a betting book on Milbury? The *ton* would find it most entertaining.

Rob rose as the man strode forward. He approached Fiona first, because this was her home and they had already been introduced to each other in London. "Lady Shoreham, what can I do but thank you from the bottom of my heart for your bravery in rescuing my sons?"

Fiona turned to Rob and, at his nod, introduced the marquess to him. "Lord Milbury, I merely sat in the boat while the duke did all the rescuing. His instincts are excellent and he sensed your boys might get into a bit of trouble the moment he spotted them. This is why we were so quickly on the scene. Any gratitude is entirely owed to him."

Milbury cast him a sincere smile. "I have heard only the finest things about you, Durham. Everyone I know speaks highly of you. But I must say, even that praise falls short. You saved my boys. Mere words cannot express how grateful I am to you."

Rob accepted the compliment with modesty. He was not usually a modest man, but he saw how close a bond the marquess had with his sons, and how sincerely humble the man was in offering his gratitude. It would not do to boast about his actions when it had amounted to little more than lifting the older lad out of the water. Timing was everything, was it not? Five minutes later, and they might have been fishing the boy's lifeless body out of the water.

He shook out of the thought.

Indeed, timing was everything. It mattered in saving lives and, to Rob's frustration, mattered in whom to marry.

At Fiona's invitation, the marquess took a chair and they all sat relaxing on the terrace while watching the sunset. It was a little after eight o'clock now and the sun would not set for another hour or two, but the colors were already breathtaking. However, they were not the fiery hues that had filled the sky last night.

Tonight, the sky was a mix of softer colors, pinks, yellows, and the palest shades of purple against the blue expanse.

"I shall not take up more of your time," the marquess said, watching his boys devour more cake. "But I would be honored if you would both join me for supper tomorrow evening. It is the least I can do. Indeed, it feels so little in repayment for saving my boys. Please accept my invitation."

Fiona glanced at Rob and waited for his nod before responding. "We shall be delighted."

"Good. Then I look forward to seeing you tomorrow."

The boys bowed to Rob and then ran to fiercely hug Fiona.

She laughed and hugged each one back. "You had better be on your best behavior from now on," she teased, "for I shall be asking your father for a full report tomorrow."

They nodded. The younger lad's smile was quite broad, since he was shorter and had managed to plant his nose in Fiona's bosom while embracing her. Truly, these boys were far too precocious for their ages.

Would their father try anything with her?

Fiona gave Rob's shoulder a light swat to regain his attention once they were alone again. "You looked like you wanted to strangle Milbury. I thought he was very nice."

"He *was* nice." But his boys were already plotting to make Fiona their mother, and the marquess did not seem very far behind in thinking to take her as his wife.

Fiona swatted his shoulder again when he mentioned it. "Do not be ridiculous."

But it seemed obvious to him. Besides, the little hairs on the back of his neck were prickling again. He hated that it was happening now. It could only mean one thing...Milbury was going to propose to Fiona.

Perhaps not this week or next, nor even next month. But it was going to happen eventually, and it made Rob physically ill just thinking about it.

Fiona must have sensed his turmoil, for she was quite pleasantly responsive to him when he joined her in bed that evening. Perhaps she also felt this was a possibility and wanted to give him more memories between them to savor over the years.

Or maybe he was thinking too much about losing her to another man, and because of this was particularly attentive—and effective—in sending her soaring to new heights.

He watched in wonder as she shattered in starlight.

This was what she called his pleasuring her. Starlight.

He did not know what to call the intensity of his own release…fire, perhaps. Maybe wildfire. Possibly a raging inferno, for this was what roared through his veins whenever he touched her and embedded himself inside of her.

No precautions taken. Just raw intensity and desire.

Nor would Fiona consider taking any precautions, because she thought herself barren.

However, each time they coupled, every time he invaded her sweet, tight core, Rob silently prayed for the miracle of conception.

He'd marry her in a trice if they were ever so blessed. He would marry her, love her to the depths of his soul, and always protect her. This was what he hoped for and had only ever wanted.

Give Fiona this miracle.

Please.

"Why so pensive, Rob?"

"Am I?" He caressed her as they lay beside each other, hot and breathing heavily after a particularly splendid coupling.

"And why are you now frowning?"

"I did not realize I was. Am I not permitted to revel a little in the aftermath?"

She leaned over and kissed him on the shoulder. "You are not reveling so much as thinking too hard about what we are doing. Don't, Rob. Especially do not get your hopes up, or this will be too painful for the both of us. Aren't you the one who always tells me to stop pondering the where, why, and how of everything? *Some things are just not meant to be.*"

He let out a heavy breath. "Promise me you will only ever

marry for love. I could endure it if I knew you were happy and had made a love match."

"You are the only one I love, Rob," she whispered, and let out a ragged breath. "I wish it were not so, for then you might be able to let go of me and move on. But our hearts are impossibly entangled, aren't they? Perhaps we were born to be bound to each other, destined in the stars, and this is the tragedy of it."

"It doesn't have to be tragic."

"We shall have this week together and you cannot ask me for more. You need to sire sons to continue the Durham line. And I... Who knows what the future will hold for me? But I know what has you worried. You think I am going to encourage Milbury to court me."

He arched an eyebrow. "Have you been thinking about it?"

"No, but you have."

He pursed his lips. "Maybe. A little."

"A lot, if I know you." She kissed his shoulder again. "I would never consider marrying him."

This surprised Rob. "Why not? He seems a decent fellow."

"Are you taking his side now?"

"Hell, no. Just speculating."

"He would have to be a fool to offer for me, especially since he must know there is something going on between us. What man wishes to embark upon a marriage thinking he will be made a cuckold?"

"Would you do this? I cannot believe you ever would. You are too honorable ever to betray him once you are married. Besides, men can lie to themselves about such things, especially when the woman they admire looks like an angel, which you do. You are a widow, so he has to know he would not be buying unsampled goods."

She pinched his shoulder. "And you think he won't care that you are *sampling* me while he undertakes his courtship? Betrayal does not extend only to marriage. How can you think such a thing of *me*? When have I ever behaved in that wanton fashion?"

She turned away in a huff.

He wrapped an arm around her and drew her up against his chest. "Truce? I don't want to fall asleep with you angry with me."

She let out a heavy breath. "I am not angry with you. I won't deny I considered Milbury as a possibility, but only as a last resort. I would consider marrying him if you stubbornly continued to remain a bachelor because of me."

He tensed.

This was his exact fear, was it not?

"You were so good with those boys today, Rob. So wise and patient, but also with just the right amount of stern authority. You would make a wonderful father. I wish this for you with all my heart."

"Then give *us* a chance to try for it."

"I've had eighteen years of chances," she said with exquisite pain.

"But not with me." Did they not deserve more than a week to see this through? Should he not have another year or two? Or five?

She said nothing in response, just cried herself to sleep, tearing at his heart.

He fell into a fitful sleep and awoke before dawn to sneak back into his bedchamber before the staff began to stir.

Carrying his boots in hand, he walked stealthily down the hall, his bare feet making not a sound upon the wood floor. This one week of wanton bliss was not working out quite as he had hoped. Only a couple of days had passed since his arrival and both of them were more on edge than ever. The toll was exacting and exhausting, both of them soaring and jubilant one moment, and then sinking into an abyss of despair in the next.

Their feelings were too raw and volatile. Their hearts were a gaping wound.

He considered ending this week early, but the thought of missing out on even a moment with Fiona made his stomach churn.

It was not about the bedroom. It was about her.

He was seated on his bed, lost in contemplation, when he heard a light shuffle at his open door.

"Rob?"

Fiona stood in the doorway, looking fragile and beautiful as the first rays of sunlight filtered into his room.

His heart swelled just from looking at her. "I did not mean to disturb you when I left."

"You didn't." She smiled. "I felt cold without you beside me."

"I'm sorry I behaved like a jealous arse last night."

She shook her head and walked into his room. "You were fine," she said, and took a seat beside him on his unslept bed, one he needed to mess up before the maids walked in to clean his bedchamber. "I was the one who goaded you. I did not mean to do it, but is it not obvious that you deserve to be a father?"

"And you? What do *you* deserve?"

"A week of happiness with you."

"That's it?"

"And hopefully a lasting friendship. Could you at least smile at me? I had no idea you were such a grumbling bear in the morning."

He gave a short, quick laugh. "I will after I have my coffee. Right now, I want to grumble and rage at the heavens for putting us in this untenable situation."

"And all will be better after you have had your coffee?" She cast him a delicate smile. "That is so *you*, Rob. But you are mostly just wonderful, even when you lumber around like an irritated bear."

"Do not flatter me and make me smile when I am about to work myself into a manly sulk. Besides, I am a panther and not a bear. Is this not what you always say to me? *Stop looking at me with your panther eyes.*" He grinned at her. "And you need to stop tossing me that beautiful smile. It is giving you an unfair advantage."

"Then I'll leave you to your moping and pouting for now, but you must promise me that you won't leave here before the week is up."

"I won't leave." He raked a hand through his hair. "You have my word on it."

Blessed saints. If it were up to him, he would never leave her.

"And promise you won't bite off Milbury's head if he smiles at me."

"All right, but no guarantees if he sets a hand on you."

She sighed. "I am not going to encourage him, so kindly do not kill him."

"This is what you told me last night," he said. "Do you really mean it?"

She nodded. "So long as you keep to your part of the bargain."

"That infernal bargain," he muttered, stretching out on the bed beside where she was seated. "What sort of ladies did you and Cherish pick out for me?"

"Smart, witty. Beautiful. But you will see for yourself in a matter of days."

"They won't be you."

"Stop, Rob. You cannot continue with this attitude."

He placed his hands behind his head as he regarded her. "Perhaps my attitude will improve after I leave here and we are no longer sleeping together."

"I hope so," she said without much enthusiasm. "Can you refer to it as something a little nicer than *sleeping together?*"

"That *was* my nice way of describing what we are doing. I could have said rutting like rabbits...or described it in far cruder language."

She smacked him on the shoulder. "No, we are exchanging hearts and creating treasured memories."

"We are *breaking* our hearts, for every day together reveals just how perfect we are for each other, and yet you want to doom us to remain apart. I want you to know one thing, Fiona..."

"Only one? What is it?"

"Your marrying another man will *never* compel me to look elsewhere for a bride. As far as I am concerned, I have found the woman I want. I am looking at her right now. All you would be doing is binding yourself to some clot you do not love."

"I don't believe you. You would have no choice but to move on if ever I married." She tipped her chin in the air and walked out.

He closed his eyes and shuddered.

Lord, he needed a miracle. How many nights of coupling would it take to bring this about?

They spent the morning taking a long ride through the countryside, both of them needing to work out their unsettled feelings and frustrations. In the afternoon, they took a long walk along the beach.

As the sun began its slow descent on the horizon, Rob knew it was time to return to the house and prepare themselves for dining at Lord Milbury's home.

Fiona mentioned the stately manor had previously been called Wembly Walk by the old owner, Lord Wembly. Milbury had renamed it Milbury Hill upon acquiring the property.

Well, things changed. Didn't they? Time moved on.

However, Rob knew his feelings for Fiona never would.

Was this not the crux of the problem? He truly believed they were destined in the stars. She even described her shattering pleasure as *starlight*.

It all had significance.

How much easier it would be for both of them if their hearts were able to move on, but how could they ever move on when doing so would cause a profound celestial break?

He turned to look at Fiona as she glided down the stairs in a gown of silvery green that had a matching wrap she'd draped casually over her arm.

She looked stunning, as always. Not in an ice princess way, either. Her smile exuded warmth and her eyes sparkled. She had dimples, too. Deep ones that had always fascinated him. Her hair was lush and silken to the touch, styled in an elegant chignon that exposed her slender neck.

He'd been careful not to leave a mark on her tender skin as he'd nibbled it last night. Quite stupid of him. He ought to have given the spot below her earlobe a light bite, behaved like a baboon and left a small irritation on the soft flesh where every other man could see it and know she had been marked by him.

She is mine. Keep your distance.

"Ready?" he asked, meeting her at the foot of the steps to escort her to his ducal carriage.

She nodded. "I wonder what he's done to the place? Poor Lord Wembly became too infirm to manage the estate on his own and allowed it to become severely run-down. It must have been close to a ruin by the time he passed on."

"Did he have no heir to help him out?"

"Oh, yes. He had several nephews just waiting for him to take his last breath, all of them worthless. The one who inherited Wembly Walk wasted no time in selling the beautiful property to Milbury."

"You just called it a ruin. How beautiful could it have been?"

"It *was* beautiful, Rob. Even with a crumbling house. The land was the asset—good farmland and a magnificent view of the sea."

The ride was short enough that Rob could have driven the two of them over in one of Fiona's rigs. But he was being a brute about it and wanted Milbury to remember that he was the duke and the marquess was below him in rank.

Truly a jealous baboon thing to do.

But so what?

The boys rushed out to greet him and Fiona as soon as their carriage drew up under the portico. Rob's ill humor faded, for these boys had a charming innocence about them, even if they were little devils and—gad, they were now discreetly leering at Fiona.

She did look exquisite. However, he would have to punch

their father if he looked at her in the same way his boys did.

Fiona subtly kicked him.

Milbury hurried forward to greet them. "You must forgive me if I seem a little out of sorts. My sister arrived today and I have been trying to settle her in. Welcome reinforcements," he said with a laugh that sounded sarcastic to Rob's ears, "for my boys have me at my wits' end. My wife was the one who took care of our children and handled all other domestic matters."

"And now your sister shall?" Fiona asked.

He nodded. "For the moment. Not certain how that will work out. Come onto the terrace and I'll introduce you to Cordelia. We'll have drinks out there and then we shall move indoors for our supper, since the gnats will eat us alive otherwise. Lady Shoreham, would you care for a tour of my home later?"

"We would love it," she replied, although Milbury had offered the tour only to her. "I can see already you have made vast improvements in the home."

"Wembly, the poor sod, had not done anything to it in almost fifty years. I considered tearing down the entire structure, but my architect assured me the bones were solid. So we've brought it up to current living standards and given the old girl an uplift. New paint. New windows and doors. Revived the floors. Fixed the leaks. Secured the roof. Got rid of the vermin. New drapery, wallpaper, and furniture."

They walked through the parlor and onto the terrace while Lord Milbury spoke about his new home. "The floors are all part of Wembly's original construction. They held up remarkably well and only required scraping, sanding, and a fresh coat of polish. Ah, here is my sister, Lady Cordelia."

Rob thought Milbury's sister appeared quite severe, as she was dressed in an unflattering gray silk gown that seemed to dull her luster, assuming she ever had any of it to start. He could not see her as a luminescent beauty even in her younger days. Her hair was also severely drawn back without a trace of style or softness.

But he bowed politely and muttered an insincere compliment. "A pleasure to meet you, Lady Cordelia."

"You as well, Duke," she intoned rather flatly, looking down her nose at him.

Yes, definitely severe.

Milbury, while chattering, had mentioned his sister was younger than him by several years. She seemed to be about forty, only a few years older than Fiona. But she looked far more advanced in age, perhaps because she was bitter and unhappy, as though life owed her more. Her hair was beginning to turn gray and her face looked sallow. There was anger mingled with resignation in her eyes, and a disapproving tension in the tight purse of her lips.

Nothing like Fiona. Fiona could have turned one hundred and thirty-eight and still had sunshine in her smile and a starlight sparkle in her eyes.

Rob gave her credit for attempting to interject gaiety into the evening, for she was lively and could talk the hind legs off a donkey if the situation required—which it did tonight, since Lady Cordelia said hardly a word as she glowered at Fiona throughout their meal.

At first, Rob chose to give the lady the benefit of the doubt and credited her silence with fatigue. But as the evening wore on, it became obvious the woman was jealous and resentful of Fiona. The few comments she made in response to Fiona's attempts at pleasant conversation were snide and condescending.

When the marquess stepped away a moment to make certain his boys had gone to bed and were not up to any of their mischief, his sister chose that moment to show her hand. "Do not expect to be welcomed here again," she told them both. "I see what is going on between the two of you. Lady Shoreham, if you believe you can convince my brother to marry you and still keep up your tawdry liaison with your *companion*, then you are sadly mistaken."

Rather than be insulted, Fiona took it quite humorously.

However, she would not allow the woman to sling her barbs at Rob. "If by my *companion* you mean this valiant duke who saved the lives of your nephews yesterday, then let me assure you that I shall never give up his friendship. Make of it what you will. But I think your brother and his boys see him clearly for the quality gentleman he is. I would tread carefully if I were you, or you might find yourself booted out of Milbury Hill before you've had the chance to unpack."

"We shall see who is the one cast out of here."

The harridan began to quote the Bible, referring to Babylon, the mother of harlots, and an abomination of the earth, all the while staring at Fiona.

Gad, the sister was a loon.

"Let me take you home, Lady Shoreham," Rob said, having had enough of this puritanical drivel, and deciding it was better to leave before Fiona no longer found the insults humorous and decided to declare all-out war on this shrew.

Perhaps Lady Cordelia would not have been so rude to another pretty woman who came to visit her brother. It could be that her venom was reserved for Fiona because of the timing of it all. Milbury was obviously interested in Fiona, and the sister, having just arrived, was not ready to have her place as lady of the house so quickly usurped.

Nor was Milbury as doting as his boys toward Fiona. But he *had* been casting her speculative looks throughout their meal. He had also been the soul of politeness toward Rob and appeared to enjoy their lengthy conversations.

However, Rob knew the marquess also had to view him as competition. To Milbury's credit, he had been an excellent host and too much of a gentleman to show him any disdain, assuming he held any. The fellow seemed decent and genuinely grateful to Rob for saving his sons.

"Yes, let your paramour take you home," Cordelia said, holding back nothing while her brother was out of the room attending to his sons. "I do believe you have worn out your welcome here,

Lady Shoreham." For good measure, she cast Rob a look of disgust. No doubt she viewed both of them as rubbish to be tossed out along with the table scraps.

Who was this wizened crone to pass judgment? Honestly, he was so tired of these holier-than-thou pillars of Society and their undercurrents of disapproval. He had precious few days left with Fiona and did not wish to waste any more evenings in unpleasant company.

Fiona was the soul of amiability as she wished Milbury a good evening when he returned. "A most enjoyable supper, Lord Milbury. But I have an early morning meeting with my estate manager and will be dead on my feet if I do not retire at a decent hour tonight."

"Ah, then I do apologize for ducking out a moment to look in on my boys. I could have left them to themselves for a short while longer while I basked in your lovely company. But I expect we shall meet again soon, for I have been invited to dine at Northam Hall next week. I understand the Duchess of Bromleigh is a dear friend of yours."

"Yes, quite dear to me," Fiona responded. "I look forward to seeing you then. As for your boys, it is wonderful they have a father who cares for them as you do."

"You are too kind, Lady Shoreham," he said, bowing gallantly over her outstretched hand.

Outside, Rob assisted her into his carriage and climbed in after her. He let out a groan and loosened his cravat once they were on their way back to Shoreham Manor. "What a spectacular waste of an evening," he muttered. "Milbury is decent, I suppose. But that sister of his—blessed saints, what a bitter, old hag."

Fiona remained silent.

He leaned forward. "What's wrong?"

"She cannot be more than five years older than me. Is this what *I* shall become?"

"You? Like Lady Cordelia?" He eased back with a shudder and laughed. "No, that will *never* be you. Not in a thousand years.

That woman was born cheerless and filled with bile. You were born smiling and sweet as sugar."

Fiona laughed. "Hardly. You know I can be quite sour at times."

"You? Sour? Never. Indignant, perhaps."

"Well, call me indignant, then. I wanted to poke her in the nose for what she said about you."

"Who cares what she thinks of me?" He arched an eyebrow. "I can defend myself, you know. I am no longer three and in need of you to come to my rescue. Although I did enjoy envisioning your leaping across the table, fists raised, ready to pound Lady Cordelia into pudding."

"It felt good to get in a huff on your behalf."

He reached over and took her hand. "You were very elegant in giving her a set-down."

Fiona laughed again. "Liar. You must have been wincing the moment I opened my mouth. But I really disliked the way she looked down her nose at you."

"I was irrelevant, and you know it. Her venom was aimed at you, for you are the real threat to her status. I hated the way she thought herself better than you."

"Oh, do not get incensed on my behalf. I rather liked being considered a shameless harlot who cavorts with younger men and gets away with it."

"Do not make light of it, Fiona. I did not like her insinuations or accusations one bit," he said in all seriousness, but made no further comment on that, since they would fall back into the discussion of his desire to marry her. "That woman borders on the deranged."

"Oh, I think it is more that she is jealous and afraid."

"Someone to be pitied rather than feared? Let's hope it is merely that."

"I think her brother realizes it was a mistake to invite her to Milbury Hill and will arrange for her departure very soon. Rob, will you have a talk with him and let him know what she said to us? Not that I wish to upset him, but he needs to be made aware what went on outside of his presence."

"All right, if you want me to."

She nodded. "I do, for the sake of his boys more than anything. It is better if he hears it from you."

The staff had retired for the evening by the time they returned to Fiona's manor. While she ran upstairs, Rob made certain to lock the front door and check the ground-floor windows and doors to make certain they were sealed tight. He knew Simmons must have done this already, but he was feeling rather protective of Fiona at the moment and saw no harm in making the rounds himself.

Out of an abundance of caution, he checked each door and window twice.

When finished, he strode upstairs and went directly to her bedchamber, for he felt the urgent need to take her in his arms. Even though Fiona had not cared about the insults hurled at her by Lady Cordelia, they had affected him on her behalf.

Fiona had donned her nightgown and robe by the time he joined her. She was seated on a stool beside the hearth, brushing out her hair and humming softly while awaiting him.

Heat and longing filled him as he watched her run her brush through those glorious tresses, and another pang of longing gripped him when she noticed him quietly standing by the door and her expression immediately softened.

"Rob? Are you all right?" She set her brush aside and rose to come toward him.

No, he wasn't all right.

He was hurting badly because he wanted to do the honorable thing by her and felt the passage of these days with an urgency that burned into his soul.

Their nights of intimacy would end soon, and he was not prepared for it.

Wordlessly, he shut her door and lifted her into his arms to carry her to bed.

CHAPTER SEVEN

R OB'S PANTHER EYES were piercing as he stretched out on the bed beside her, his expression intense and territorial, silently proclaiming that this was where he belonged.

Not for the length of a week. He was demanding to be here every night for the rest of their lives.

She could have hurled back a string of reasons why he needed to marry someone else, but she had neither the heart nor the desire to lecture him. Instead, she gave herself over to him as he undressed her and made fierce love to her.

Once. Twice.

Intense. Scorching. Unmistakably devouring. Untamed. Clothes off and bodies entwined.

With each kiss and embrace, he proclaimed his love for her. As sure as the sun rose every morning. And as surely as the silvery moon marked the impending night.

She wanted to cry a thousand tears for the impossibility of it all. How could something beautiful ever spring from their coupling? She would have begged, pleaded, crawled on her knees if only it would do any good.

She closed off her painful thoughts and gave herself over to his exquisitely gentle touch. Would her skin feel so soft or her breasts fill the cup of his hands so perfectly if they weren't meant to be a match?

Would their souls have been cut from the same bolt of celestial cloth if they were not destined to be together?

Her heart beat so strongly for him sometimes, she was certain it would pound through her chest.

He made love to her a third time as dawn approached, no doubt feeling a physical ache at the thought of their separation. But he had to leave her, or her servants would talk.

Not yet.

A few more minutes. They still had a little time before the traitorous dawn stole him from her side.

They took no precautions, enjoying each other without limitations, since there was no risk of her conceiving. Rob had readily agreed to this careless arrangement, because what did he have to lose? Nothing at all, especially if she were proved wrong and found herself with child.

She saw the hope in his eyes. Then he would gain everything. The wife he wanted. A child, no matter whether a boy or girl. Only a son could inherit his title, but how was this a problem once it was shown she could be fertile? They could always try again for a son if their first was a daughter.

If only this were possible. But what were the chances?

Nil. Impossible.

Fiona's eyes began to tear.

Noticing this, he rolled off her and brought her along with him as he rested on his back. She nestled within the circle of his arms. Were they making a terrible mistake by indulging in this week-long love fest?

She wasn't feeling very festive. Nor was he.

This was what worried her most. Were they working toward a happy outcome? Or merely making their inevitable heartbreak worse?

Fiona drifted off again, and opened her eyes to find the morning sun brightly shining upon her face. Rob must have opened the drapes for her before he left her bedchamber, because it was still too early for Molly to come in and wake her.

Feeling unsettled, she tossed on her robe and padded across

the carpeted floor to peer out the window, not surprised to find Rob striding from the stable toward the house after his morning ride. This had become his routine these past few days.

She enjoyed riding, too. But their nighttime frolics had left her sated and shamelessly lazy. These nightly activities were new to her and quite exciting, but they also took an overwhelming toll with each coupling.

It was not only because Rob's body was flawless and the scent of him divine. Nor was it merely that his arms were the perfect amount of strong and solid, and she particularly enjoyed falling asleep while wrapped in his muscled embrace.

She would have enjoyed waking in his arms, too. But he was always careful to leave her bed before anyone in the household stirred.

Having him all to herself this week had filled her with dreams and possibilities, but she knew allowing these feelings to slip into her heart was dangerous. The entire point of their seven days together was to gorge themselves on each other and be done forever.

But it was having the opposite effect.

Rob glanced up and smiled upon seeing her at the window. "Good morning."

She smiled back and waved. "I'm meeting with my estate manager this morning. Care to join me?"

"Does this mean you weren't just making up an excuse to leave Milbury's home last night?"

She shook her head. "All real."

"Sounds fun. Sure."

"You don't have to if you don't want to. I only mentioned it because you usually like this sort of thing. You always had a good head for business."

"I do wish. What time are you meeting him? And is he coming here?"

"No, I'm meeting him at the farm. Nine o'clock sharp."

"All right. Let me wash up. See you in the dining room in half an hour."

Once he disappeared into the house, Fiona went to her wardrobe to select a suitable gown to wear for inspecting a farm. She withdrew a dark-gray muslin, momentarily thinking of the drab gown Lady Cordelia had worn last night, and how hideous she looked in it.

Fiona sighed and shook her head as she stared at her reflection in the mirror. "You are nothing like that disapproving crow."

So what if it was not her prettiest gown? Rob always looked at her as though she were the most enchanting vision alive.

Oh dear. She was going to cry again if she allowed her thoughts to stray to him.

Firming her resolve, she donned the gown that had been designed for functionality and was easy to slip on and off.

Molly came in just as Fiona was putting on her sturdy working boots, so there was little left to do but assist with her hair. "And help me with this necklace, Molly."

"Oh, m'lady. It is lovely," her maid said when Fiona showed her the lapis lazuli gem now held on the thin gold chain. "I noticed you wore it yesterday, too. Mind you don't lose it in the muck."

"I'll be very careful with it."

Molly grinned. "Oh, I know what you are about. You want that luscious man to see you wearing his gift."

Fiona laughed. "I am merely being a polite hostess."

"Right, m'lady. If you say so. Is it just me or is he getting handsomer by the day? My eyeballs haven't stopped rolling in their sockets since he carried the neighbor's injured boy back to the house. Never seen a man look so good shirtless. Thick, solid muscles. Broad shoulders. Tight stomach. Poor Gladys is still walking around cross-eyed after a glimpse of him."

Fiona sighed again. "He *is* spectacular, isn't he? Quite handsome when he smiles."

"Which he does all the time now. He is happy being around you. His entire expression softens whenever he sees you. And that devastatingly handsome smile of his is pure heaven. Have you noticed how it shines through his eyes when he is around you? I'll bet you make him smile a lot at night, too."

"Molly!" Fiona tipped her chin in the air. "I wouldn't know about that."

"Oh, is that so? Do you think I cannot tell he has been warming your sheets? Probably warming some rather unused parts of your body, as well."

"Molly!"

"Well, I hope they are being put to good use. That man could set a woman on fire with merely a glance. But I know he's been doing far more than glancing at you. He probably knows tricks that would make a sailor blush."

Fiona rested her elbows on her vanity table and groaned. "I refuse to talk about him."

"You needn't say a word. The blush on your cheeks tells me all I need to know." Molly let out a long breath. "M'lady, please think about what you are doing."

"I don't know what you mean."

Molly cast her a gently stern look.

Fiona relented. "I can do nothing but think of him, and each time I am led to the same conclusion. This has to end. For his sake, he has to move on and marry someone able to give him children."

Molly gave her a hug. "But this is his choice to make, not yours. He is fully aware of your situation and you are not deceiving him in any way."

Fiona's stomach began to churn. "I never would lie to him." And was she not obligated to prevent him from making the biggest mistake of his life?

She changed the topic of conversation, knowing there was no point to dwelling on the hopeless situation. "Please advise Simmons I'll need the rig brought around."

"Right away, m'lady." Molly nodded and then bustled out.

Fiona walked downstairs soon afterward, her heart turning

light and breezy when she saw Rob seated at the table nursing his cup of coffee. He was frowning, lost in his thoughts and looking quite daunting, for anyone who did not know him would have thought twice before approaching him when he wore that serious expression.

However, he rose and managed a smile as soon as she walked in. "Good morning, again."

"Did you wait for me before digging into the salvers?"

He nodded. "Didn't want to be rude and start without you."

"Nonsense, you must be starving after your morning ride. Did you enjoy it?"

"Yes." He shot her a look that revealed he had enjoyed their night rides, too.

Heat shot into her cheeks.

He cast her a knowing grin.

Dear heaven. He needed to behave or her entire staff would know how they had been spending their nights.

Well, they probably did anyway. Molly certainly knew.

Eager to leave the house and be away from prying eyes, Fiona shoveled down her eggs and kippers, finished her tea, and then rose. "Time to go."

"All right." Rob had gobbled down his food, too. But this was only because he had seen her move fast and realized she wanted to set out for the farm as soon as possible.

The rig was ready and waiting for them when they walked out the front door. Rob helped her climb in, and then took the driver's seat himself.

With a crisp flick of his wrists on the reins, they were off.

However, the simple ride proved something of a dilemma, for their shoulders constantly grazed, reminding Fiona how nicely broad his were.

Molly's cautionary words this morning came back to haunt her. Was it truly Rob's decision alone to make about whom to marry? Did she not have a say in it, too?

And was it not also a Crown matter? The Durham dukedom,

a historic title and bastion of power in England for almost a thousand years, was at stake. Would Rob be permitted to throw it away?

Everyone else seemed to think it was not of major concern. How easy it would be if she simply went along. Unfortunately, she could not, for along with the benefits of their status in Society came responsibility.

Fiona's sense of duty had been ingrained in her since childhood, and she knew that she had to do the right thing. Was she not obligated to steer Rob correctly, especially if he was inclined to make the wrong choice?

She diverted her attention to her own affairs when the farm, which comprised a vital part of her wealth, came into view. It was only a twenty-minute ride from Shoreham Manor, and was a profitable enterprise that gave her a steady income. It also provided employment for numerous local families.

She looked upon the farm as her child in many ways, for she was responsible for the welfare of everyone who depended upon it for their livelihoods. Shoreham had given it to her as a bride gift upon their marriage and left the running of it entirely to her and his competent estate manager, Mr. Sykes, an amiable man in his early fifties with a full shock of white hair.

"Good morning, m'lady," Mr. Sykes said, hurrying out of the barn to greet her upon hearing the rattle and rumble of her rig.

"Good morning," she replied, smiling at the older man who had run the Shoreham holdings for almost thirty years, and her own bride gift for these past twenty years.

She introduced the man to Rob, who offered his hand in greeting. "A pleasure to meet you," he said with sincerity. "Lady Shoreham speaks of you with tremendous respect."

"Well earned," Fiona added.

The estate manager gave a humble smile. "Well, I do my best, Your Grace. And it has always been a pleasure to work for Lady Shoreham."

He then led them on a tour of the farm. Of course, Fiona

knew it well. But she was curious about what Rob thought of the operation. In all the years she had owned the place, she had never brought her guests here. Mostly because those who came to her house parties were all about having fun, not stomping about in muck or watching sheep being sheared.

But Rob was avidly interested in all aspects. Soon, he and Mr. Sykes were engrossed in conversation as they walked across the fields, their heads bent toward each other, unaware she had slowed her step and lingered by the sheep pens to allow the pair to talk at length about livestock and arable land.

Since she was so familiar with the place, any problems were easy for her to spot and assess without the need for her estate manager to point them out. Fortunately, there appeared to be nothing major to address at the moment.

However, this did not mean she could sit back and not concern herself with the farm. Constant vigilance was required, and constant maintenance as well. She took note of the wood beginning to rot along the sheep pens, but that repair could be delayed until next spring. She would ask Mr. Sykes for his opinion.

The odor of chickens wafted from the coop as the light breeze shifted and sent their pungent aroma her way. She heard their clucks and squawks, and the low bellows of her milking cows as they were led out of the barn by one of the farmhands into the lower pasture.

Being so close to Brighton was an advantage, especially as the town became more popular with summer visitors. There was always a need for eggs and milk, and their prices held up well due to this demand. The farm also had an apple orchard that provided apples in the autumn and cider throughout the winter.

Fiona was quite proud of this property.

She also did not regret having married Shoreham, for he had been kind and generous with her, and was this not enough of a blessing in one's life?

Plus a week of delicious sin with Rob? Her nights with him had felt particularly decadent because he was so adept in the bedchamber. And she did not hold back in her responses.

Perhaps she would have felt less sinful had she not known him since childhood. Yet, at this point in their lives, the six-year difference in their ages did not seem quite so impossible.

It would have been nothing had Rob been the one who was six years older.

But he was certainly old enough now, no longer the little boy who used to follow her every step, or greet her at the door like an adorably excited puppy whenever she came to visit with her mother.

Dear heaven. He had grown so impossibly handsome and completely dangerous to her heart.

She shook out of her thoughts when the men strode back from the pasture to join her. The three of them walked to Mr. Sykes's office, where they reviewed the ledgers and made decisions on what to repair next.

One entry made her frown. "Is Mr. Holland no longer purchasing his eggs and milk from us?"

Mr. Sykes nodded. "He claims our prices are too high and he went elsewhere."

"That is ridiculous. Our prices are set at market rates. What is going on with him?"

"I don't know. His son was the one who approached me and instructed me to stop deliveries to his father's bake shop."

"*That* weasel? He's going to stint on quality and destroy his father's business before the year is out. I'm not going to let him get away with it."

Rob glanced at her with his eyebrows arched. "Does this mean you want to take a trip into Brighton next?"

He knew her so well. "Yes. Do you mind?"

"Not at all. I am entirely at your service."

Mr. Sykes laughed as he turned to Fiona. "You are going to box the son's ears, aren't you? Be careful. The man is a no-account and will not behave like a gentleman."

Fiona tipped her chin up. "I'll flay him alive if he tries any-thing. More important, I must talk sense into Mr. Holland. He cannot let that worthless son of his run the bakery into the ground."

"Is it not the baker's business what he wishes to do about his son and his shop?" Rob asked.

"No, it is mine because he is a customer of ours and his son will have him bankrupt and begging on the streets if someone does not step in to stop the damage."

"Is his son merely a wastrel, or is he dangerous?"

"Merely a wastrel, I'm sure. He's too lazy to get off his rump and actually do anything."

But Rob noticed the small hitch of hesitation in her voice. "Perhaps you ought not—"

"I'm going. Will you come with me, or shall I have Mr. Sykes hitch his own rig and take you back to Shoreham Manor?"

"I'm going with you, of course. You know I am not letting you walk into trouble on your own."

"Shall I come with you as well, Lady Shoreham?"

Rob stepped in and answered for her. "No, Mr. Sykes. I am fully able to protect her, and she will need someone trustworthy to run the farm when I am proved wrong and the son takes a shotgun to us."

"He's a conniving weasel, not a murderer," Fiona assured him, although this did not seem to mollify him very much as they climbed back in her rig, bade her estate manager a good day, and proceeded to Brighton and Mr. Holland's bake shop.

"You could have left the matter to Mr. Sykes," Rob men-tioned as they turned onto the main road leading to Brighton.

"No, the responsibility is mine. Besides, the son will not re-spond to a commoner, but he will not dare cross a countess." She glanced at him. "And he will cower when he learns you are a duke."

"We could go back to Shoreham Manor and use my car-riage."

"No, you do not need your lion crest emblazoned on the door to show your authority. You carry it just fine on your person alone. You really are wonderfully daunting and authoritative."

He laughed and gave a shrug. "All right, but I want you to stay behind me when we walk into Mr. Holland's establishment."

"Why? It isn't an army garrison, just a bakery. The only powder floating around will be the flour one uses to bake. However, I do appreciate your desire to protect me."

"Oh, I don't think you do," he said with a note of seriousness. "I can already see that you plan to leap out of the rig and barge into the store the moment we arrive. But you must wait for me to go in first, Fiona. You are little and slight, and will be the first one hurt in a brawl."

"There isn't going to be a brawl. Good grief, do you think this is how I deal with my wayward customers?" Although she did have to calm down and approach the situation with more circumspection and less bellowing. "I cannot talk to him if I am cowering behind you. But I do promise to stand close by you."

"We'll see about that."

They said nothing more to each other, but Rob's silence was worrying her. He could not be overset about this unexpected trip to Brighton, nor seriously worried about a wastrel son who was probably purchasing inferior ingredients for cakes and pies, could he?

This ran deeper, and was likely about them. Of course. Did he think she was not taking him seriously?

Goodness. He was *all* she thought about. If only she could dismiss him from her thoughts. But he was constantly in them, filling her heart and her every waking moment to the point of obsession.

She wanted him so desperately. Giving him up would be the hardest thing she would ever have to do in her life.

"Did you notice I am wearing the necklace you gave me?" She forced a cheerful smile.

He let out a breath and chuckled. "I notice everything about you."

Oh.

He was bringing the conversation around to them again. She needed to divert him. "I wonder if Mr. Holland has taken ill. His son would never be able to take control otherwise."

"Sounds probable."

"Shall we stop for ices after we've addressed the baker problem?"

"If you wish."

She was going to ask him what he wanted to do, but feared he would respond, "I want to head to the church and marry you," and she did not have the strength to hear more of that today. Was she not feeling just as much pain about their situation as he was?

And now her stomach was feeling heavy and beginning to cramp because it was coming upon her monthly time. "Never mind. No ices. We had better go straight home after the bakery."

He glanced at her. "Why the change of heart?"

"I'm not feeling at my best just now."

"What's the matter?" He drew up on the reins. "The baker and Brighton can wait for another day. Shall I take you straight home?"

"No, let's finish our business first. I'll be fine. Truly, Rob. Do not treat me like a delicate porcelain doll."

He eyed her warily but did as she asked.

The baker's son was seated outside the bake shop when they drew up in front of it. Rob hopped out immediately, and then came around to assist her down. "Is that him?"

"Yes," Fiona whispered. "Look at his slovenly appearance. His apron is dirty. His father would never allow this if he were here." She peered into the bakery to confirm the father was not inside. "What is going on here, Holland?" she demanded, steeling her spine and tipping her chin up to look every inch his superior. "Did your father authorize you to change suppliers?"

The baker's son rose slowly and cast her an insolent glower. "*I* run this establishment now. No one tells me what to do."

"Where is your father?"

"The shop isn't his anymore. Ye're not to bother him, m'lady."

"That isn't what I asked you. Where is he?"

The son shrugged. "Home."

She turned to Rob. "We can walk there. He lives close by."

Rob did not look pleased, either. But Fiona could not ignore a longtime customer. What if the man needed her help?

She marched around the corner to a small house just off the high street and knocked on the door. The baker himself answered, and he did not appear to be suffering at all. "Mr. Holland? Why is your son in charge?"

"Good morning, m'lady. Is he already giving you headaches? I was afraid this might happen, but did not expect it so soon. You see, I gave the shop over to him just last week."

"Why? You do not look ill. What happened?"

The man gave a jovial laugh. "Indeed, I am in the pink of health. But I've amassed a tidy sum over the years and thought I would do a bit of traveling while I had the chance. I gave my son the shop and this house. It is all his to tend now, although you and I both know he will lose everything within the year if he does not change his slovenly ways. But that is his lookout now. He's full grown and has never done anything for himself in his life. It is time he learned."

A pretty, older woman came from his parlor to join them at the door. Fiona recognized the butcher's wife, who was recently widowed, although she did not look much like a grieving widow. "Mrs. Fallow?"

"Would you care to come in, my lady? And you, good sir? You are most welcome as well. I shall put on the kettle for us."

Fiona shook her head. "Thank you, but we are in a hurry. However, I wanted to make certain Mr. Holland was all right."

"Very kind of you, m'lady," the widow said, smiling up at the baker. "We shall be traveling together. Pooling our resources for this next adventure. I daresay we are both well and happy."

Fiona let out a breath. "Then I wish you a most pleasant

journey, wherever your hearts may take you."

After exchanging a few more pleasantries, she and Rob walked away. "Wipe that smug grin off your face," she said.

He held out his arms as though innocent. "What did I do?"

"You are giving me that 'I told you so' look and silently chiding me for meddling in the baker's business."

"You *were* meddling, but you were also concerned for him. I'm glad his story had a happy ending."

She nodded. "Yes, but his son is a toad and will destroy everything this man has built up over a lifetime of toil."

"It happens to the best of us, Fiona. Wastrel offspring are the bane of too many families to count. Wealth and title does not spare them from the ills of stupidity or sloth. Look at my own family. How did we come to this end? I am the last surviving male heir when there ought to have been five or six in the Durham line ahead of me and another two or three after me. Of the ones who came prior, not one of them died honorable deaths. One drowned, another died in a duel, two of them fell off their horses and broke their necks because they were reckless or drunk, and another died of an unnamed disease probably caught while in a brothel."

He sighed and shook his head. "That does not even take into account the Durham men in my grandfather's generation. He had three brothers and a host of male cousins. I suppose some of them died honorably on the field of battle and others simply died natural deaths from old age. But they had more than their share of scandals."

"Not you, however. You were perfect, Rob. You have never taken a step out of line. I've never met a smarter man or one with better common sense and noble valor. You behave honorably at every opportunity."

He ran a hand through his hair in consternation. "You call this love fest you and I are indulging in nightly honorable?"

"Yes."

He laughed. "If you say so. But I don't think my sticking

my…myself in you at every opportunity is something I wish to boast about."

"Are you ashamed of me?"

"No, you know I am not."

"There is nothing wrong with what we are doing, Rob. We are doing this because we…" *Love each other and are desperate for a solution.* "Because we care for each other and want to do the right thing. That means moving on with our lives."

He cast her a look that warned he was not ready to move on.

But he would have to be.

She said nothing until they were back in the rig and on the road to Shoreham Manor. The sun was at its full height and the breeze had stilled to nothing.

Heat beat down on them, making her wish they had stopped for ices. But this was out of the question now, because they were too far outside of Brighton. Besides, she really needed to get home. She placed her hand on her stomach as the cramps became worse and made her want to double over. She would soon start bleeding, which meant Rob would not come into her bed and there would be no more nightly romps.

Not that any of their love endeavors could be called romps when their hearts were so deeply engaged.

She knew this news would break his heart. He was so certain love could fix everything, that his potent seed would leave her with child.

Perhaps in a perfect world this might happen, but they lived in a world that was often cruel and unjust. The simple truth remained: she was broken and could not be fixed.

Perhaps now he would understand this.

She gasped as the carriage wheels hit several ruts in a row and made her insides lurch. Now her stomach was cramping painfully.

"Oh, hell. Fiona, we've hit a bad stretch, but we'll reach smoother ground in a moment. Did you hurt yourself when we bounced over that last rut?"

"No. It isn't the ruts."

He studied her, his expression one of worry. "Then why are you crying again?"

CHAPTER EIGHT

ROB'S HEART PHYSICALLY ached when Fiona told him the reason for her tears. "My monthly courses, Rob."

He'd known disappointment before and had faced harsh circumstances, but seeing Fiona so undone truly broke him. Simply cut him to the quick.

"This is a minor setback," he said, wrapping an arm around her and drawing her close as they rode together in the rig.

She viewed the onset of her monthly bleeding as proof she wasn't worthy to be his wife, as though this was the only important requirement in a marriage. What did she expect him to do? Go off and bed a dozen lasses and marry the first one he got with child?

Sometimes, he just wanted to take her by the shoulders and shake her till her teeth rattled.

Despite her protests, which were quite weak and ended swiftly, he joined her in her bed that night and the next nights following, for what sort of man would he be if he left her side when she was suffering?

In truth, it surprised him just how strong some of her cramps had been, consuming her almost to the point of vomiting. Until this moment, he had not realized there was anything beyond some inconvenient bleeding that kept a woman confined to the house for three or four days.

"Is it always this bad for you, Fiona?"

"Not always," she had told him. "Some months are worse than others."

They hadn't coupled, merely shared the same bed, falling asleep with his arms around her, and then he'd crept back to his own chamber just before daybreak, each time angry and frustrated that they had to keep up this farce when all he wanted to do was be with her to comfort and protect her. It tore him up inside that he could do nothing to ease the pain caused by her own body.

Their week was now up.

He had wanted to talk Fiona into giving him another year or two with her, for he was merely in his early thirties and had plenty of time to father a son. But she was adamant that their time was up.

And now they were about to head over to Northam Hall and settle into rooms there for Gawain and Cherish's week-long house party.

"Aren't you eating?" Fiona asked on their last morning together as he sat quietly staring into his coffee and not bothering to fill his plate with the usual eggs and kippers.

"Not hungry."

She eyed him curiously. "Rob, you are always hungry."

He grunted as he stared down at his empty plate. "Yes, usually. But not today."

"Because our week is up," she said with a nod.

"It doesn't have to be, Fiona. Give us another chance."

What was so special about the debutantes who would arrive at the Bromleigh house party for the sole purpose of catching his eye? Would they be so different from next year's crop? Or those of the following year?

Fiona now had that stubborn look on her face. "You are only prolonging my misery. Do you think this is any easier for me? I am so sorry we remained friends into adulthood. Had I known how we would grow to feel about each other, I would have avoided you at all costs. At least you still have the hope of a family, so do not throw this away."

She set down her fork with a clatter, for he had upset her once again.

"Fiona—"

"No! Can you not see how this is destroying me? You cannot continue to treat this matter so lightly, Rob."

His eyes widened in surprise. "How can you accuse me of giving this situation no attention? It is *all* I think about, day and night."

"Then stop thinking about it. Stop being unrealistic and stubborn." A tear rolled down her cheek. "I would give anything for what is right there in front of you to grab. Children. A family. Stop treating this blessing that is within your reach as though it something you can casually grab at any time. It is not trivial. It is *everything*, and you must never take it for granted."

He had never looked less forward to a party. "All right. But I think *our* chance for happiness is just as important. I am taking none of it for granted. What I am doing is fighting to have all of this with *you*. Believe me, it would be so much simpler for me if I did not love you to the depths of my soul."

He took a deep breath and continued. "There is no sunlight without you. Nor moonlight to shimmer upon the gentle seas. There is no music, no flowers, no laughter. No *starlight*. None of it without you."

She emitted a soft cry.

But he was not about to relent. "I want another three years with you, but I know you will never agree to it now. So I will only ask for the three days you still owe me, since our week was cut short."

"Seriously? You are going to hold me to something that is natural to a woman's body and completely out of my control?"

He was not a petty man and would never have quibbled were it not their future at stake. "Yes, I am. This was our bargain and I am entitled to three more days of your body."

"Fine," she said with a huff. "Then come back to me after

Cherish's house party is over. You shall have your bargain fulfilled, and then you must walk away. You *must*, Rob. The thought of our parting is already unbearable for me. I cannot think of what it will do to me if we were to part after years together."

"I know," he said softly.

"In the meanwhile, you must get to know the young ladies who will be at the house party. That you might come back to me to complete our bargain does not relieve you of the obligation to look for a proper wife."

"All right," he said, knowing she was deluding herself if she believed anyone but her would ever be a proper wife to him.

His heart was heavy as he packed his belongings and made ready to leave Fiona's home later that afternoon to ride next door to Northam Hall. He realized the chunk of lapis lazuli stone was still in the drawer with his undergarments, so he tucked it in his pocket for now. He would give it to her upon his return to Shoreham Manor.

Fiona had promised she would ride to Northam Hall later today. "I have a few things to finish up here, since I will be staying with Cherish for the week. I think it is unnecessary for me to move in there, but I suppose she will not hear of my riding back and forth each day, even if our homes are on neighboring properties."

Rob was grateful for that. "Did I not express the same concern? It is the only sensible thing to do."

"I know. You've already warned me of the danger of returning home in the wee hours of the morning when highwaymen might be about."

Rob climbed into his carriage. "I'll be waiting for you at Northam Hall."

"Don't. I'll get there in my own good time. You had better be paying attention to the young ladies hoping to meet you, or I shall kick you to Brighton and back," she warned.

As the carriage rolled away from Fiona's home, Rob eased

back against the squabs and emitted a wrenching groan.

Why did his heart have to be so true to one woman? And why did that woman have to be Fiona?

Gawain and Cherish hurried out to greet him when he drew up to what had been Cherish's home before she married Gawain. They had kept the house as their summer retreat and fixed it up after her vile uncle had practically destroyed it.

The ogre had done it for no other reason than sheer spite.

Gawain gave him a hearty slap on the back. "Reggie and Margaret arrived just before you, and are upstairs unpacking. Potter," he said, referring to Cherish's faithful butler, "will see you to your room. Then come down to the study and share a brandy with me and Reggie before you face the onslaught of young ladies eager to meet you."

"And while you share that drink with my husband," Cherish said jovially, "try to convince him not to pair Fiona with Lord Pershing in our party games."

"Seriously? You invited Lord Pershing?" Rob laughed. "Bromleigh, you are evil."

Gawain arched an eyebrow. "Turnabout is fair play. Fiona put me through hell by sticking me with that sot at her house party last year to make certain I would come in last in every game. Meanwhile, she was handily winning every round because she had you, Reggie, and Cherish on her team."

"It served you right," Cherish teased. "You were so busy trying to foist Reggie on me, when we were clearly an incompatible match, that she had to make you suffer a little for your own manipulation."

Gawain gave her a kiss on the forehead. "Will you listen to this, Durham? Chided by my own wife."

"Well, it all worked out in the end," Rob said, smiling. "Did it not? You both look happy as larks. Marriage obviously agrees with both of you."

Gawain put an arm around his wife's waist and nodded. "Never happier."

Rob had to agree with that assessment, for Cherish seemed to be glowing. In truth, there was a radiance to her, and she had put on a little weight that suited her beautifully. But he shrugged off the thought as Potter led him upstairs to his guest quarters, a nicely decorated room obviously designed for male guests—unlike most of the house, which had a bright, airy seaside feel.

This chamber with its polished, dark wood wainscoting and large bed anchored by a dark wood footboard and headboard suited him perfectly. The carpet was a deep blue shot through with threads of silver in a *fleur-de-lis* design. The windows looked out onto a landscaped garden and the sea beyond.

He expected Cherish would give everyone a tour of the house that she had refurbished with such pride over the course of the year, but this would likely wait until more guests had arrived.

Since no one was to know he had been staying with Fiona this past week, Rob pretended to have come over from Devonshire, where he had conducted his most recent piece of business. He did not bother to feign fatigue, since he knew that he looked too well rested.

He quickly washed up from his nonexistent trek and headed downstairs to the study, where Gawain and Reggie were waiting for him. Reggie was another newly married friend who also looked ridiculously content.

"Gad, I never expected to be the only bachelor among us," Rob remarked, sauntering in and taking one of the comfortably padded leather chairs beside Reggie. "Am I going to see this same silly grin on Margaret's face?" he teased. "Marriage agrees with you."

Reggie laughed. "Amazingly, it does. Margaret is wonderful and sweet as anything. You ought to try this marriage business. It has worked out quite well for me. For Uncle Gawain, too."

Rob accepted the drink now handed to him. "I'll keep an open mind about it."

"You had better," Gawain warned. "Cherish and Fiona have been giving the downfall of your bachelorhood much consideration."

"Not to mention the betting book out on you at White's," Reggie said. "The *ton* is in a frenzy wagering over whom you will marry."

"Bollocks, do not remind me." Rob turned to Gawain and scowled. "Are you going to deny that you and your Silver Duke friends were the ones who opened it, Bromleigh?"

"I have no intention of denying that we set up that betting book, but we never meant for the attention to fall to you. We were thinking of Fiona."

Rob leaned forward. "Fiona? You were betting on *her* marriage prospects?"

"That was our first thought, since she's my cousin and I love her. I want to see her happily settled. But that idea was quickly cast aside. The club members at White's refused to permit us to place wagers on a lady. So we changed the terms of that betting book, and it soon became all about you. Anyway, Fiona is not yet ready to marry, despite any rumors to the opposite effect. As for you, I think you will like the ladies Cherish and Fiona have chosen for you."

Rob forced a smile. "I am sure they are all lovely."

Gawain laughed. "I might believe you if you did not look as though you were being led to the gallows."

Rob shrugged. "Can you blame me? I do not enjoy this attention being foisted on me. Did you like it any better when you were one of London's most sought-after bachelors? And a Silver Duke, no less."

"I will admit, I detested all the attention." Gawain nodded. "But that unwanted interest in my every movement was a small cost, considering all the benefits gained from inheriting the Bromleigh title. You are the Duke of Durham now, and that comes with responsibilities. You need to sire heirs to continue the line and protect all those who rely upon your care. And before you lace into me for my resisting this very task into my forties, let me point out that our situations are not quite the same. I had a capable heir," he said, glancing at Reggie, "who would step into my place when the time came. You have no one, Rob."

"I know." Wasn't this what Fiona had gone on about this entire week?

"Margaret thinks you are going to like the choices Cherish and Fiona have made for you," Reggie said, frowning slightly. "She says they are all smart ladies."

"Then why the furrowed brow?" Rob asked.

Reggie raked a hand through his hair. "It was the way Margaret stated it, claiming they were much smarter than her. She is so quick to dismiss her own intelligence or the many other fine qualities that make her a wonderful person. It wasn't her fault that her parents saw no purpose in educating her."

"Cherish adores her," Gawain said. "I expect she, Margaret, and Fiona will be thick as thieves throughout the week, no doubt plotting to get you to the altar before summer's end."

Rob winced. "That's what I am afraid of."

"Well, you might like their choices," Reggie said. "Fiona is especially clever about this matchmaking sort of thing."

Yes, he knew.

Rob drained his glass and rose. "Mind if I take a walk before the others arrive?"

Reggie rose along with him. "I'll go with you. I need to stretch my legs as well."

Rob had wished to be alone, but Reggie was always good company. He had been a trusted friend for years, and it would not hurt to confide in him if ever he felt the need.

Not now, of course. Nothing had happened yet.

But all hell would break loose at some point.

Fiona was determined to match him with one of her hand-picked choices, but how would she react when she saw him paying attention to any of these young ladies? Fiona felt things so deeply. How was she going to respond if he led one of these hopefuls into the garden for a turn around the flower beds? Or danced a waltz with any of them?

Well, there were no answers to be had just now.

The pair made their way outdoors while Gawain returned to Cherish's side to assist her in greeting more new arrivals.

"Do you know who they plan to foist on me?" Rob asked as he and Reggie wandered among the well-defined paths that were a mix of lush foliage and floral blooms in a blaze of summer colors.

Reggie nodded. "I think they chose well for you, avoiding this year's crop of *ton* diamonds because they felt these debutantes were too young for you. They were certain you would dismiss them as peahens."

"Good. I do not want to be listening to some eighteen-year-old goose going on about whatever nonsense comes into her head."

"Ease up, Rob. You are barely in your early thirties and would not be considered too old even for the freshest debutantes. Nor are they all so witless that you would consider them inane and boring."

"I am not saying I would…only that I probably would."

Reggie shook his head. "Most of them were raised as Margaret was, lacking in academic education. Since Fiona and Cherish consider you particularly intelligent, they sought out bluestockings for you. Ladies in their twenties who had experienced a couple of London Seasons."

"And who might those bluestockings be?"

Reggie gave him a friendly poke in the ribs. "Gad, Uncle Gawain was right. Stop looking as though you are about to be marched to the gallows."

Rob laughed. "Sorry. I'll try to do better."

Reggie studied him a moment longer. "I know these ladies are not Fiona. But give them a chance, won't you? You need to get over her, because she will not marry you."

Rob's heart lurched. "Why do you mention Fiona?"

"Oh, I don't know. Perhaps because you light up like a chandelier whenever she is present. You are hopeful of making a match with her, aren't you? But it will never happen, Rob. No one wishes the circumstances were different more than I. You know I love you both dearly. I also think you are a perfect complement to each other, for you are the solid anchor she sometimes needs to keep her firmly grounded, while she is the spark to jolt you out of your set ways when you become too serious."

"And your point in telling me how right we seem to be for each other?"

"By pressing your suit, you will only cause her anguish. If you love her, as I know you do, then let her go."

Rob felt as though his heart was being ripped out of his chest. "Message received, Reggie." He stalked off because he needed to be alone to recover his composure.

Everyone, even Fiona herself, was insisting he move on.

He thought so, too. But thinking to do it and actually doing it were completely separate matters.

Why couldn't even one of his feckless male relatives have left a legitimate male offspring to succeed him? Was it asking too much? Those worthless knaves had spread their seeds everywhere except in their own wives' bedchambers.

He wandered down a small path that led toward an open field dotted with wildflowers to his right and some woodlands to his left.

A flash of light amid the trees caught his attention, and he decided to investigate the source.

In truth, these small rows of trees hardly qualified as woods and were more of a glade than an actual forest. They were slender, easily bending in the strong winds that often swept to shore with the warning of a storm. Their barks were a stark white and their delicate leaves a silvery green that shimmered in the sunlight and shivered upon a light breeze.

He saw the flash of light again, this time closer.

"Hello?" he called out. "Anyone out here?"

There was a flutter amid the leaves as several birds must have been startled by his shout and flew away.

In the next moment, a young woman dropped down from one of the trees only to land as softly as a cat upon the grass directly in front of him.

"Smartly done," she grumbled, intending no compliment. "You've chased away the birds."

"My apologies," Rob said, wondering who she was.

She did not appear to be a trespasser, not with the impudent tip of her chin or the withering look she shot him, as though he were the one infringing here.

"Who are you?" he asked, his tone perhaps more gruff than necessary.

It was no polite way to greet the young lady, but she seemed capable of holding her own. "Who are *you*?" she retorted.

"I asked first."

Her gaze raked over him as she assessed him, as though she were trying to determine whether he was a gray speckled sparrow or a pied woodpecker. Finally, she stuck out her hand as though expecting him to shake it as he would a man's.

He considered merely bowing over it in courtly fashion, then decided against it because she did not seem to be the sort of young lady who would appreciate the polite gesture. So he just stood there awaiting her answer.

She sighed. "I am Florence Newton, a friend of Jocelyn, Duchess of Camborne."

"Ah, then you must be the bird-watcher friend she's told us about." Since her hand was still extended, he shook it. This felt odd because he was not in the habit of taking a firm grip on a woman's hand. "I am Robert Durham, the Duke of Durham. A pleasure to make your acquaintance."

She cast him a wry smile. "You're the poor wretch they are all trying to match at this house party. Is this why you have run off already to hide in the woods?"

He laughed. "Yes, you have found me out."

She eyed him speculatively this time. "Do you like birds?"

"To eat? To hunt?"

"To admire," she replied. "Do you really shoot them?"

"On occasion. I also eat them from time to time. And you?"

She nodded. "I am guilty of feasting on quail or game hen on occasion. Unfortunately, it is one of the necessities of life in order not to starve. But birds are such beautiful creatures and so graceful in flight."

"Is that a sketchbook tucked under your arm?"

She drew back a step, as though worried he might reach for it. "I like to draw them, and I take notes on their nests and nesting habits. I happen to be chairwoman of the Ladies Ornithological Society in Lower Bramble. Have you heard of it?"

"The bird society or the village of Lower Bramble?" Rob asked, finding Florence Newton a little eccentric but amusing. She wore spectacles, had nondescript dark hair, and her gown was buttoned to her throat.

Yet she was not unattractive.

"Either one," she replied.

"No." He studied her prim gown that was obviously well made but designed for practicality rather than allure. The color was a dark brown, no doubt chosen to blend in with the surrounding woods. This might have worked had the tree barks not been a stark white here.

"Lower Bramble is one of the lovelier villages in Devonshire," she said.

"I see. I was just there on some Durham estate business." He offered his arm to escort her back to the house, since she appeared to be done with her bird watching for the afternoon.

She ignored his offer and simply walked along beside him.

He liked this independent streak in Florence.

Was this perverse of him? To prefer a lady who did not cling to him like a mouse and declare him to be perfectly wonderful?

Fiona knew his likes and dislikes almost better than he did himself, and he could see why she'd chosen to invite this particular young lady.

Well, this was Cherish's house party, but Fiona had certainly played a major role not only in the menu planning but in the selection of suitable young ladies.

"Durham," Lady Florence said with a matter-of-fact air as they walked along, "you needn't worry that I am after you. In truth, I am only here as a favor to Jocelyn, and to avoid being hounded by my own family. But I have no intention of marrying a man like you."

That stopped Rob in his tracks. "What do you mean by that statement?"

"Please do not take this as an insult…"

Which he did.

"But you seem quite tightly wound and come across as the sort who will never take a toe out of line. That can get awfully tiresome."

"And you know this about me how?" Being serious and attentive to duty were traits one should hope for in a husband, were they not? He was not tightly wound, as she had just accused. However, he did like to be in control of his feelings and actions. Was this not better than being an out-of-control arse?

Nor was he averse to taking a toe out of line. She had only to ask Fiona about the nights he'd spent in her bed.

He raked a hand through his hair in dismay, for this was not something ever to be discussed with anyone but Fiona herself.

"Well, it has been a pleasure talking to you, Durham. Do not bother asking me to dance or partner you in cards for the duration of our stay. I am not good at either and will only frustrate you, since you are obviously a man who strives for perfection and likes to win."

With that, she scampered into the house.

No wonder Florence was still a spinster despite her decent looks and quick wit. Some might call it an outrageous wit, for she had spent much of their walk insulting him. A duke. A desired bachelor. And she would not stop tossing him barbs.

But if she truly had no desire to marry, then she might be useful to him over the course of the week.

He walked onto the terrace, intending to stroll into the parlor, but was waylaid by a friendly summons from the Duke of Lynton, who had just arrived and immediately stepped out for air on the terrace. His wife, Eden, stood smiling beside him.

"Durham, good to see you again," Lynton remarked. "How have you been?"

Rob arched an eyebrow. "Not as happy as you, by the look of it."

Eden cast him a gracious smile. "Are you ready for the onslaught? You won't be the only eligible bachelor present, if that is any consolation."

"Oh, gad. You are not referring to Lord Pershing, are you?"

Eden shook her head. "Well, he may be eligible and a bachelor, but I would hardly call him a prize catch. But I understand Viscount Aubrey will also be in attendance. He is an avid bird watcher and—"

Rob laughed. "Ah, I see where this is going. You think to match him with Florence Newton?"

Eden appeared surprised. "How did you know?"

"Good luck with that," he muttered. "Have you met her?"

"No," she admitted. "But Camborne's wife is best friends with her and has assured us she is lovely. Do you know her?"

Rob grinned. "I've only met her briefly. She is…different."

Lynton chuckled. "Uh-oh. That does not sound promising. Do you think she will give Aubrey a hard time?"

Hell, yes. "I'm sure he will find her…endlessly fascinating."

Lynton appeared gleeful.

Eden gave her husband a swift poke in the ribs. "Don't you dare give me that attitude."

Rob excused himself and moved on, not wanting to get between those two, who were about to bicker. Not that Lynton looked at all put out by his wife's not-so-subtle reprimand.

He heard them laughing together only a moment later, so their disagreement was not in the least serious.

Rob met Viscount Aubrey about an hour later. He had gone

to the stable to see about borrowing a horse in order to ride over to Fiona's home to see what was delaying her arrival, and found the viscount also hiding out there.

Rob strode over to greet him. "Always nice to meet another fox about to be hunted down. I'm Durham," he said, extending a hand.

"Ah, the duke everyone is agog over." Aubrey grinned. "My sympathies on that betting book commenced on you at White's. Trajan Aubrey, a viscount by courtesy title only."

"Your father has just inherited a dukedom, I've been told."

He nodded. "Yes, he's the newly minted Duke of Weymouth, and this has now catapulted me onto the list of London's most eligible bachelors. I might be the next target of that loathsome betting book. Hopefully not for a while yet. However, the Duchess of Lynton is determined to introduce me to some bird-watching spinster," he said with obvious dismay.

"Ah, you mean Florence Newton. I've just met her. She's a bit of an odd duck, to be sure. However, I think I like her."

"You only *think* you like her? I'm not sure what to make of that remark."

Rob shrugged. "And I'm not sure what to make of her yet. She isn't impressed by titles."

Aubrey arched an eyebrow. "That is a point in her favor."

Rob casually leaned his shoulder against one of the stalls and folded his arms over his chest. "She wasn't impressed by me at all."

That made Aubrey chuckle. "Perhaps she will find me equally unimpressive. One can only hope."

"You do not sound eager to find yourself a match," Rob mused. "Why attend this party if you're not interested?"

Aubrey's grin faded. "I don't know. Just stupid of me, I sup-pose."

Hell. Was this man still pining for Lynton's wife, Eden? No wonder Lynton was peeved to learn he would be joining them for the entire week.

Rob and Aubrey were quite a pair of bachelors, weren't they? Two fools pining over women they could not have.

Did he look as pathetic as Aubrey looked right now?

At least Fiona was unmarried and still available, although she could stubbornly go off and marry some clot she did not love if he played this wrong. So he needed to be certain his plan would lead her to the right result.

He also needed to hope Fiona would not see right through his motives and move to counter them.

Reggie entered the stable, interrupting their discussion. "There are the two holdouts. I thought I might catch you in here. Bromleigh's looking for you both."

"Why?" Rob asked, feeling rather surly.

"Fiona has arrived."

"Let the games begin," Rob muttered, striding out to face this week-long agony.

CHAPTER NINE

AFTER A LATE breakfast the following morning, Rob stood on the terrace of Northam Hall with Gawain and Reggie, the three of them looking on as they watched Fiona, Cherish, and Margaret engage in lawn games with the other house party guests. He was pleased to see Reggie much matured and proving to be of great help to Gawain in managing the Bromleigh properties. Apparently, marriage was good for some men.

Reggie had married Margaret a little over three months ago and seemed quite besotted with the sweet girl. But she was still a bit of a peahen, not that Rob would ever admit this to his best friend.

Margaret's strength was that she had the kindest impulses. She also clearly adored Reggie, who needed a boost in his confidence from time to time, especially whenever he was around his uncle, the imposing Duke of Bromleigh. Reggie idolized the man.

And Margaret thought the sun and the moon revolved around Reggie. This unconditional adoration was something Margaret provided her husband simply by loving him whole-heartedly and believing he was the most wonderful man alive.

But love seemed present everywhere at Northam Hall, for Gawain was also completely enamored with Cherish, his gaze constantly on his wife as she participated in a game of archery.

As hostess, Cherish had organized her guests in teams, and

points were to be awarded for every game. The team who had the most points at the end of each game was to be given a prize. The team amassing the most points by the end of the week was to receive a grand prize.

Just what that grand prize was, no one knew yet. Cherish would not reveal what it was.

As Rob watched, he saw that teammates Margaret and Cherish were demolishing their competition. Fiona, who had been partnered with Lord Pershing, did not look happy at all. In fact, her expression was murderous.

Not that Rob blamed her, for Pershing was already deep in his cups and it was not yet noon. Fiona was doomed to take last place in every event while burdened with that wastrel on her team.

"You are a terrible influence on Cherish," Reggie remarked in jest to Gawain. "She is as ruthless as you and Fiona at these games, not to mention she is turning Margaret into a competitive beast with killer instincts. We should not have allowed them to team up. They are showing no mercy to the others."

Gawain laughed. "I shall be content so long as they beat Fiona's team. Stomp on them. Rout them. Annihilate them."

"Uncle Gawain!" Reggie tried to appear disapproving, but Rob heard his friend's chortle and knew he was just as eager to see Fiona defeated.

They loved her, of course. Fiona, Gawain, and Reggie were family and quite close knit. But Fiona and Gawain were both competitive and could be ruthless on the field of play.

Well, Rob knew he could always step in if Fiona needed his help. But she was scrappy and knew how to fight for herself in most instances.

As for Gawain, he was out for good-natured revenge in retaliation for the team Fiona had saddled him with during her own house party last year. However, he would never take it beyond a friendly feud. This was Gawain's chance to exact harmless revenge, for this was his turf now and his rules would apply.

Even Rob could not help laughing as he watched this archery competition play out. And what could be a more fitting revenge than to have Cherish and Margaret, the two sweetest and gentlest ladies at this party, defeat her?

"You invited Pershing just to stick him on Fiona's team, didn't you?" Reggie accused his uncle. "Lord, he's so drunk, I'm surprised he is still standing. I ought to go over and take his place. He is going to shoot someone through the eye with his arrow, probably himself. The man is utterly useless. He has yet to hit a single target."

Gawain stopped him. "Fiona is about to strangle him with his own bow. I cannot wait to watch this."

Rob could not suppress a burst of laughter as he watched Fiona chase Pershing around the lawn. "You are cruel, Bromleigh. When are you going give Fiona a reprieve?"

"Perhaps tomorrow, but not yet. I am enjoying this too much." Gawain grinned. "Pershing is too drunk to keep running for long. He'll pass out soon. I'll rescue him before Fiona actually strangles him.

"Oh, hell," he said a moment later. "Cherish is going to rescue him. Botheration, I had better get down there before she ends up with a black eye."

Rob followed because he wanted to protect Fiona on the chance Pershing lashed out at her.

Gawain was two strides ahead of him as they raced onto the lawn. "Love," he said, reaching Cherish and immediately placing a protective arm around her waist, "you are in no condition to be mixing it up with those two."

"Fiona knows my condition and will be careful around me," she assured him.

Her *what*?

Rob's heart sank as he overheard the pair talking.

No, it could not be. Perhaps Cherish had recently been ill and this was all her husband meant by telling her to take it easy and not step between Fiona and Pershing.

"But Pershing doesn't know," Gawain insisted, lowering his voice. However, his whispers still reached Rob's ears. "You are only four months along and hardly showing yet. I will have to kill him if he hurts you, accident or no."

Rob let out a pained breath. Gad, what an idiot he was. Cherish was with child…and had just assured her husband that Fiona knew and would be careful not to harm her. Which meant Fiona must have been given the happy news either last night or earlier this morning.

His heart broke as he studied Fiona. How was she taking it?

Of course, she would be ecstatic for the pair. But she had to be secretly aching.

Cherish cast her husband a loving look as he kept an arm around her. "Gawain, you are being apishly protective again. But very well. For the sake of saving Pershing's life, go ahead and separate those two before Fiona knocks out one of his teeth. You know how competitive she is, so why torment her? You are having far too much fun with this."

"It is nothing to the agony she put me through last year. Although she did find me my perfect match, so I suppose I ought to be grateful. All right, I'll put Durham on her team tonight."

He turned and gave Rob a grin as he strode closer.

"He's a very smart fellow," Gawain added, knowing Rob could now hear every word between husband and wife. "They'll win every game once he is on her team. Will this make you happy?" He gave Cherish a lingering kiss, and then ran off to haul Fiona off Pershing, who was sprawled on the grass and not moving.

Rob followed him, just because he felt the need to be close to Fiona.

"He looks dead," Gawain muttered. "You didn't kill him, did you, Fiona?"

"No, but it isn't for lack of trying," she grumbled. "I can hear him snoring. Just leave him there. He is in no one's way and will eventually wake up on his own. I hope it rains on him."

Gawain glanced up at the sky that was a deep, cloudless blue. "No rain today."

"Too bad." Fiona refused to look at Rob, no doubt sensing he understood her turmoil and the true reason behind it.

He followed her as she returned to the other guests to finish the archery game her team could not possibly win, since Pershing had just forfeited his turn.

"Come take a walk with me, Fiona. The game's over," he said a few minutes later as Cherish and Margaret were declared the winners, received their prizes—a little bow-and-arrow bracelet charm for each—and the players began to disband.

"No," Fiona said, her lips quivering. "I'm tired."

"Then come sit with me."

"You'll want to talk, and that will only make me cry."

"I'll do my best not to say a word and let you do all the talking."

"Rob," she whispered in utter anguish, "just leave me alone."

How could he when he knew how badly she was aching?

But he sighed and glanced up at the noonday sun beating down on them. "All right. Care for a lemonade? It's hot out here. I'll fetch it for you, and then you can tell me to go away."

"And you will?"

"Yes, if you still want to be left on your own."

She relented and gave a nod. He settled her in a shady spot and went off to fetch her a drink.

Along with hers, he poured one for himself before returning to her side.

"Stay, Rob," she said, looking ready to talk once he handed over her glass.

He sank into the chair beside hers, nursing his lemonade while waiting for her to start the conversation.

"Cherish and I are as close as sisters," she said after taking a sip of the refreshing libation. "How could I not be overjoyed for her? She asked me last night if I would be godmother to their child."

"Did you accept?"

She let out a ragged breath. "Yes, of course. She and Gawain will reveal her delicate condition to the others once she starts to show in another month or two. Meanwhile, they would prefer to keep it quiet and share the news only with their closest friends."

"I won't say a word," Rob assured her.

Perhaps he wasn't meant to know yet, but Cherish and Gawain had not tried very hard to keep it a secret from him.

"Do you want to hear something hilariously ironic?" Fiona said, letting out another shaky breath.

Rob's heart sank. "What is so amusing?" However, he knew by the quiver of her lips that it was not at all funny.

"Margaret suspects she may also be with child. But it is very early days yet and she cannot be sure. She hasn't even told Reggie because she is afraid he would be crushed if it turned out to be a false alarm."

Blessed saints.

Both of her dear friends with child?

He knew Fiona was happy for them and only wished them well. But the news had to be as painful as a knife plunged through her heart.

Rob did not know what to say.

Fiona cast him a wistful smile. "I'll be all right. Do not worry about me."

He wanted to sweep her into his arms and hold her so very tightly, absorb her into himself. Of course, that was physically impossible, but could he not at least absorb some of her pain?

Yet here he was. Unable to comfort her or do anything for her at this vulnerable moment.

Worse, she wanted him out of her life. His every thought and instinct was to remain close and protect her. How could he ever walk away when he knew how much she was suffering? And would he not be causing her more suffering by pretending to consider someone other than her as his wife?

Frustration roared through him.

He noticed Aubrey watching them.

So did Fiona. She drew away. "Go and mingle with the young ladies in attendance. They are a clever lot and quite pretty in their own quiet way."

She scurried off, giving him a look that warned he had better not follow her.

Aubrey approached him as he sat staring with misery into his glass of lemonade. "Seems I am not the only lovesick fool, Durham. You might be even more of a fool than I. Frankly, I did not think it was possible."

Rob grunted in acknowledgment and set his drink aside. "Bad situation."

"They are right, you know," Aubrey said, settling in the chair Fiona had just vacated. "We need to move on. It isn't easy. Quite hard, in fact. But I am determined."

Rob shrugged. "Do you have a choice?"

"No, clearly I do not."

"What are you going to do about it?"

"I thought to approach Florence Newton. I find her surprisingly intriguing. Quite pretty if you get past her spectacles and hideously unstylish gown. But she cast me such a withering look the moment I took a step toward her that I went off to the stable again and simply had a chat with my horse."

Rob laughed. "You could have chatted up some of the other young ladies."

"Yes, I know. But I thought to start with Florence, since I enjoy a good puzzle. She is an odd duck, just as you said. I have yet to figure her out."

"I'm sure she pushes us away on purpose."

"I cannot blame her. We are not exactly prize catches at the moment," Aubrey said. "There are three other young ladies here who seem promising. Have you spoken to any of them yet?"

"No," Rob admitted. "But I will this evening."

"Who will you approach first? There's no point in both of us going after the same young lady."

Rob shrugged. "I'm not going after anyone just yet." *Or ever.* "How about you? Have any of them caught your eye, Aubrey?"

"Florence did, but she is now at the bottom of my list."

"Ah," Rob said with a nod. "An intriguing puzzle but not a prospect for marriage."

Aubrey grinned. "I have no intention of marrying someone who will do nothing but cast me withering looks. Should there not be a glimmer of affection even if there is no love match?"

"Well, you both share a love of birds. Perhaps she will warm up to you because of that."

"I'm not sure what she's doing," Aubrey said, frowning, "but she isn't watching birds."

The remark surprised Rob. "Seriously? What do you think she is up to, then?"

"I have no idea. Spying on someone, perhaps. Bird watching is just a ruse to allow her to march around with binoculars in hand and not raise any suspicions."

"Truly?"

Aubrey nodded.

Rob scratched his head. "She had me fooled. She claims to be chairwoman of some fancy ornithological society in Lower Bramble."

"And who's to question her?" Aubrey snorted. "Who knows if the society or the village even exist?"

"Truly? Do you think something clandestine is going on with her? Should I say something to Bromleigh? This is his home and his party, after all."

Aubrey shook his head. "No, I don't think she is going to cause trouble. In all likelihood, she concocted this bird-watching ruse to give herself an excuse to march off into the woods whenever convenient to avoid unwanted attention from the eligible bachelors. That she walks around with her binoculars could just mean she wants a wider view of her surroundings so she can see us coming from a distance and run off before we find her."

"I see." Yes, that was the most likely reason.

"Quite clever of her, really," Aubrey mused.

Rob agreed.

"Ah, look," Aubrey said, pointing toward the lawn where the contestants had been playing archery a short while ago. "Pershing is awake and now wandering off in the wrong direction. Perhaps I had better go after him before he stumbles into the pond and drowns."

But Gawain must have been thinking the same thing, for he sent one of his footmen after the wastrel to escort him back onto the terrace, where others had now gathered for cakes, tea, and lemonade.

Fiona was among that crowd, smiling and chatting away as though she were having a grand time.

Aubrey smacked his hands to his thighs and rose. "We had better join them before our hosts come after us with hatchets. There's an open seat by Lady Eloise Barclay. I think I'll start there. What about you, Durham?"

A gentle breeze blew off the water and rustled through the trees that provided them a most comfortable shade where they were seated. But Rob rose, too. "I'll start with Lady Millicent Randall."

"Why? Because she is seated closest to Lady Shoreham?"

Actually, he had not been thinking of that at all.

Or perhaps he had been doing so unconsciously.

"All right, scrap Lady Millicent. I'll start with Lady Anne Hastings." Gad, she looked to be not at all promising. Yes, she had lovely golden hair that shone a rich hue under the sun, and very pretty blue eyes that appeared to have a small depth of intelligence, but there was a smugness about her that put him off. She knew she was beautiful and expected this to be enough for any man.

Or perhaps he was merely being peevish because Fiona was forcing him to look at other women when he only had eyes for her.

"Did you enjoy this morning's lawn games, Lady Anne?" he asked a little later, trying not to look reluctant as he settled beside her.

"Yes, quite. But you did not join in, Your Grace."

"I preferred to stand back and watch you lovely ladies."

Was this not the tritest line? He really needed to put more thought into his conversation.

But the young lady seemed to preen under the compliment. "Then you are forgiven," she said, flashing him a flirtatious smile.

He strained for another topic. "Have you been to the Brighton area before?"

"No, this is my first time."

"And how do you like it so far?"

"Well, it seems a bit isolated. And the breeze off the water is a constant nuisance, isn't it?"

"A cooling breeze is a good thing in the summers," Rob remarked. "Otherwise, it can get quite hot, especially as the noonday sun beats down on you."

"Yes, there is rather a lot of sun out here. Perhaps the Bromleighs should not have organized so many outdoor activities for us. It is not good for a lady's complexion. And the constant wind makes it impossible to keep one's hair properly styled. One has only to look at the Bromleighs' neighbor, Lady Shoreham, to see what the ravages of time in this place have done to her."

"She looks fine to me," Rob muttered, doing his best to stifle his annoyance.

What in blazes? Why was this girl singling out Fiona?

"Her cheeks are too pink and will burn if she does not keep herself out of the sun. She is getting to that age where wrinkles will come fast and never disappear. For this reason, she has to be careful. And just look at her hair, all wild curls, and none of them properly held in place. But I suppose this is what happens when one is a widow and left with independent means. She has no need ever to remarry, so why bother maintaining her looks?"

"I see nothing at all wrong with her."

"Perhaps your preference is for an earthier appearance on a lady, one whose aspect is more like a farmer's wife than a countess," she said, casting another barb at Fiona.

What was it with these waspish ladies? First Cordelia Milbury and now Anne Hastings.

Rob crossed Lady Anne off his list. Being educated and considered a bluestocking was no guarantee of charm. Frankly, the young lady did not strike him as being all that bright.

But she was a schemer for certain, and might have sensed he held Fiona in some affection. Why else would she have tossed out that insulting comment?

He doubted any of Fiona's servants would ever tattle about what had transpired between him and her, and especially never utter a word to anyone working for the Hastings family.

But the *on dit* around London at one time had been that he fancied Fiona. It was also known that she had rebuffed him, although they had remained on friendly terms.

It was obvious this arrogant young lady was seeking to raise herself in his esteem by tearing down Fiona. He knew Fiona would never have done anything so cruel to this young woman.

Rob could not wrest himself away from Anne fast enough.

He moved on to Lady Millicent Randall, no longer caring that Fiona was still seated beside the girl. "May I join you?" he asked, casting Lady Millicent a rakish smile.

The girl blushed. "Yes, of course."

He settled between Millicent and Fiona, but pushed his chair back a little so that he did not interfere with their ability to see each other while the three of them engaged in conversation.

"Lady Millicent was telling me all about the new exhibits her father has sponsored at the British Museum," Fiona said, obviously hoping to get a chat started between him and the girl. "Her father is quite the archeologist and has several teams digging for relics in the area of ancient Babylonia. Is this not fascinating?"

"Quite," he said, not really feeling any excitement for the topic. Nor was he feeling anything for the girl, but he had yet to give her a chance. Also, he had to admit that this was a far more interesting subject than the weather, how to cure colic in one's horse, or which modiste a young lady ought to use when ordering stylish gowns for her debut. "Do tell me more about these new exhibits."

To her credit, Millicent went on to describe her father's hunt for places and objects rumored by lore to exist or actually spoken of in the Bible in fascinating detail. She spoke so cleverly that Rob perversely ruled her out as too clever for him.

Not that he was a dullard by any stretch of the imagination.

He called Aubrey over, thinking he might be interested not only in the discussion but in the girl herself. Millicent obviously wanted to travel the world and continue her father's work. Aubrey could do with getting away from England for a while and putting some distance between him and the Duchess of Lynton.

Fiona frowned at him when she caught on to his encouragement of Aubrey.

He ignored her frown, for he was doing nothing wrong. Millicent wanted to travel to far-off lands. He was a duke with responsibilities to his subjects and the Crown. Those responsibilities required him to remain solidly anchored to England.

Besides, he had already spent years touring Italy and Greece before the war, and then slogging through Portugal, Spain, and France during the conflict. He was done with all that and more than happy to set his roots here and never leave.

Aubrey, who was a duke in waiting, was the perfect one to undertake such travels as Millicent described.

Unfortunately, Aubrey did not appear interested either.

"My father has just inherited the Weymouth dukedom but is not up to the task of managing it on his own," he explained when Rob raised the matter with him a short while later. "Most of the responsibility has fallen upon my shoulders. Not that I mind at all, since I detest being idle. Oh, look. Our Florence has gone off with her binoculars again."

Rob had not been thinking of the young lady at all, but obviously Aubrey was still paying close attention to her. "Are you going to follow her?"

"I don't know," Aubrey said. "Maybe. I am curious about what she is doing. However, Bromleigh's wife has devised a scavenger hunt for us that is about to start. We are to partner the ladies. She will flay both of us alive if we disappear now."

"Shouldn't Florence be participating?" Rob asked.

Aubrey nodded. "But I don't think any of the other young ladies will mind her absence. Less competition for them as they fight to gain our notice. By the way, what did you think of Anne Hastings?"

"Why do you ask?" Rob did not like the way she had demeaned Fiona, but she might have gotten that bit of bile out of her system and been nicer to Aubrey.

"She spoke quite unkindly about Eden, commenting with disdain about her hair." Aubrey grunted. "How is Eden in any way responsible for the natural color of her hair? And who says red is unsightly? Eden's is a warm, dark cinnamon that suits her perfectly."

"She demolished Fiona, too." But Rob laughed at the nonsense she had spouted. "Said she would wrinkle if she did not stay out of the sun. She also claimed her hair was too wild."

Aubrey grinned. "Ah, yes. What man could possibly adore a wild mane of hair on a lady? Florence actually has nice hair."

Rob hadn't noticed.

"But those binoculars…and I also wonder whether she really requires her spectacles. She looks awfully sharp eyed to me. Maybe it's the distinctive color of her eyes, those flecks of amber mixed in with the green. Quite striking, really."

Dear heaven. He had paid *that* close attention to the color of Florence's eyes? "Aubrey, you do realize your mind is completely taken up by her."

He looked appalled. "Not at all, but is she not a distracting puzzle?"

"If you say so."

"You know what," Aubrey said, slapping his thigh, "I've changed my mind. I'm going to find her and bring her back in time for the scavenger hunt. I want her to be my partner."

"I don't know that we are given the choice. I think Cherish has already designated our partners."

"Then tell her to change mine to Florence. You will do this for me, won't you, Durham?"

"Yes, of course," Rob said with a nod, for who was he to interfere with the course of true love…or puzzle solving?

CHAPTER TEN

ROB STRODE OFF to find Cherish and relay Aubrey's request, because the hunt was going to start very soon. He approached the crowd gathered on the lawn, but could not find Cherish among those milling about.

Fiona appeared to have taken charge of this scavenger hunt game and was about to start calling out the pairs. "Make sure Aubrey gets Florence," he whispered in Fiona's ear.

"But I had her paired with you."

"Don't. Aubrey wants her."

Fiona's eyes widened as she stared up at him. "He does?"

Well, not really. But Fiona did not have to be told that Aubrey's reasons were other than romantic. She did not have to know that he was convinced the girl was doing something other than bird watching and was curious to discover what it was. "Yes, he's quite smitten."

"Truly?" She let out a breath and smiled. "Eden will be thrilled for him. She hoped he would find someone to make him happy."

"Obviously, it is early days yet," Rob said, careful not to overdo it. "But it looks promising."

Fiona's smile broadened. "That is a good start, and all anyone can ask. But Rob, I'll have to give you the young lady with whom he was to be paired."

"All right. Who is that?"

"Lady Eloise Barclay."

He nodded. "That works. I have yet to make her acquaintance. This will be a good opportunity. How long is the scavenger hunt expected to last?"

"About three hours," Fiona replied.

"Good, then she and I will have time for a long conversation."

"Excellent," she remarked, her smile turning a little *too* bright. "I have only spoken to her briefly, but she seems lovely."

"Is that so? Then I shall look forward to getting to know her better."

She tipped her chin into the air. "Yes, do."

He noticed Fiona's upraised chin begin to wobble as though she were going to cry.

In truth, he was not surprised. This had been a difficult day for her, first finding out about Cherish being in the family way and possibly Margaret, as well. Then to see him willing to escort another lady around, even if it was at *her* urging, was still a bitter pill for her to swallow.

"Fiona," he said gently, "you are the one who is pushing me to do this."

"I know. But I sincerely want you to meet these young ladies."

"Then why are you frowning at me?"

"I am not frowning," she said while doing exactly that. "I am ecstatic for you, so do not try to wriggle out of our agreement."

"Yes, I can see how genuinely you are smiling," he said with sarcasm. "Go ahead, call out our names and let's get on with this game."

Since he was to spend the next three hours in the company of Lady Eloise Barclay, he hoped she would turn out to be tolerable.

He had to admit, Cherish and Fiona had not done badly in selecting these ladies. Only Anne was an outright mistake so far, a snake in lamb's clothing, or whatever the expression. The point was that she was sneaky and not to be trusted, something Fiona would have spotted immediately had she spent any time in her company. Perhaps Cherish had been the one to choose her, for Bromleigh's wife was far more trusting and gullible than Fiona.

Their choice of Millicent was not a bad one, however. Unfortunately, Millicent was an adventuress—intelligent and thoughtful, but meant for a man who also had the desire to explore exotic lands.

Florence was quirky, smart mouthed, and independent. In truth, she reminded him a little of Fiona, and he liked Florence because of this.

But he dismissed her as a possible match because she did not have Fiona's warmth, and this was a must for him. If he took a wife for himself, she needed to be someone he could trust to love and protect their children with all her being.

That was Fiona. It was not Florence.

And now, he was to learn about Eloise.

Or not, he realized when greeted with a tepid smile from this *ton* beauty.

She did not appear pleased to see him, and actually retreated several steps as he came to stand by her side now that everyone had been matched to a partner and instructions were given out. There were eight couples paired off and eight of each scavenger hunt item hidden in the woods.

"Eight items on this list. Not so bad," he remarked, hoping to put Lady Eloise at ease, for she did not look particularly excited to be participating in this game.

She gave him a blank stare.

"We are only required to find one of each." He cleared his throat, and then continued when she made no remark. "For example, the duchess has hidden eight eggs painted pink, but we must only take one to put in our basket. If we come across another pink egg, we must leave it for another couple to find."

She still said nothing.

"Shall we start?"

She nodded.

He groaned inwardly. Did the girl forget how to speak?

He knew she could, for he had heard her chatting with Fiona earlier and laughing at one of her jests. The pair had been quite relaxed and seemed to be enjoying their conversation. But Eloise seemed to be terrified of him.

No, not terrified. Dismayed? Bored? Revolted by him?

Well, he had no idea what was going through her mind.

"So," he continued, as though this was not agony for him, as well, "we are to be on the lookout for a pink egg, a teacup, a lace handkerchief, a lady's glove, a man's snuff box, and…" He allowed his voice to trail off, since this was getting him nowhere. "How shall we approach this hunt, Lady Eloise?"

Her eyes widened. "What do you mean?"

Ah, she speaks. "Well, some of the items might be hidden under a bush and some might be found up in the trees. Shall I look high while you search low?"

"All right."

"Everyone has scattered in all directions. Is there any spot you would like to search first?"

"I shall follow your lead," she said, her voice pinched.

Was she scared of him? And for this reason sounded like a timid mouse?

Since most of the couples had started their search off to the right, he chose to go toward the left side of the woods because the underbrush was sparser and the scavenged items would be easier to spot, assuming any were planted there.

He easily found a pink egg and held it up with glee. "Success, Lady Eloise! We've got the egg."

Fiona would have laughed and perhaps done a silly dance to partake in his cheer, but Eloise just looked at him with a blank expression.

She was a bluestocking, right? Supposedly intelligent, right?

Could have fooled him.

He stuck the egg in the basket. "Right, let's move on."

It was not long before he spotted a bit of white lace caught on a twig on the low-hanging branch of a tree. "I thought I saw something in the tree, Lady Eloise." He pointed upward and feigned excitement. "Do you see it? Shall I lift you up to reach it?"

She backed away as though he were an ogre intending to do her harm.

He sighed. "Never mind. I'll get it."

Fiona would have shoved him aside, climbed the tree all on her own, her legs flailing and arms outstretched to grab the item, and then given a victory shout.

"Two items found," he said with mock enthusiasm. "What shall we look for next?"

"You decide."

"I see you are agog with excitement," he muttered, and decided to search for the teacup next. "Of course, we should also keep an eye out for the remaining objects."

It did not take him long to come upon a teacup.

"Good, we are almost done," Eloise remarked dryly.

In truth, they were not even halfway to finishing.

He paused in his next search and turned to face her. "Are you not enjoying this game? It is harmless, and an easy way for us to get to know each other. Forgive my bluntness, but it seems you wish to be anywhere but here. Is it me? Or is it just this game you dislike?"

She let out a breath. "Shall we speak bluntly?"

"Yes. In truth, I would just like you to speak, since you have hardly said a word to me all afternoon."

"I am not trying to be difficult."

Oh, really?

"I am only here because my parents disapprove of my hopes, wishes, and desires. They are pushing me toward you because you are a duke."

"There's a surprise," he said with disdain.

"They are convinced your title is all the prize I need. Let me assure you, it is not. Nor can I turn my heart on and off at will."

"Your heart? Have you fallen in love with someone else?"

Please, please. Yes.

Fiona could not blame him for a failed match if Eloise was the one who rejected him. That would neatly take care of all the young ladies they had chosen as potential matches for him, and leave him free to enjoy the rest of this house party unburdened.

"Becoming your duchess," Eloise said, regaining his attention, "and having others grovel at my feet will not lessen the pain of giving up on my dreams."

"I am not in the habit of encouraging anyone to grovel."

"I'm glad to hear it."

"Nor will I lock you in a dungeon."

"I never thought so. You do not come across as cruel. However, you do not come across as scholarly either."

Was she calling him an idiot?

He smothered a grin. Fine, let her believe he was all muscle and no brain.

"Let us clear the air, Your Grace. I do not dislike you. In fact, I appreciate your efforts to be polite and engaging. But you do not strike me as a man who will ever accept anything less than complete faithfulness in his wife, and I can never promise you this."

"You would cavort with other men?"

Holy ham hocks. That was quite the admission, especially from a girl who had hardly spoken a sentence to him in over two hours.

"Other men?" she said, the notion seeming to catch her by surprise. However, she did not attempt to deny it. "Perhaps, but I was thinking of my first love, which is scientific research and my general thirst for knowledge. They will always come first in my heart, you see."

"And what of children?"

"What do you mean? Whose children?"

"Yours. Ours if we were to marry."

Eloise blushed. "But this is why I am being honest with you from the start. I do not want the distraction of children."

"No children? Ever?"

She nodded. "That's right."

His heart tightened, for Fiona had been in anguish and praying for a child for years while Eloise could probably pop them out year after year and did not care a fig.

One of life's cruel ironies.

Eloise pursed her lips and frowned. "Nor do I want any other duties required of a duchess. My heart is pledged to learning. This I can do without interference because I have a sizeable inheritance from my maternal grandmother. Nor will my parents be excessively put out, because I have eight brothers and sisters who will be far more amenable to doing their bidding."

Rob was not so sure her family would be so easily assuaged. "Lady Eloise, they have thrown you in my path because they know your status as a duchess will not only provide a good life for you but also elevate the chances of your siblings to make good matches. Surely you understand this."

"Oh, yes. I do understand this is their aim. However, it does not seem fair of me to use you in this manner when I have no intention of taking on the duties of a wife. Well, not to a man such as yourself. And please do not take this as an insult. I only mean that you are the sort who would want a wife who understands the importance of putting your marriage first."

Was that such a demanding request? To love and honor one's husband? To respect one's marriage vows? He would do no less for his wife.

"If you must know, I would sooner choose Lord Pershing than you."

Rob shook his head. "*What?* That man is utterly lacking in moral fiber."

"Yes, I know," she said, finally smiling. "But his uncle happens to be one of the directors of the British Museum and one of the wealthiest men in England. Yes, Lord Pershing is a miscreant in every respect. But this is what makes him the perfect choice for me. He cannot get his hands on my funds because of the way my grandmother set up my inheritance."

"So, you are going to use him to get close to his uncle and further your scholarly pursuits?"

"Aren't these Society matches all about using each other to further one's goals? You will easily find someone else to marry you. Any other woman in England would leap at the chance to be your duchess. But as for me, I would rather have Pershing."

He let out a breath. "I am most grateful for your honesty."

She eyed him curiously. "Yes, I see that you are. You are taking this news exceedingly well. In truth, you look relieved. Does this mean you are in love with someone else?"

Rob was not going to answer that. It was his turn to remain silent.

"And she is denied to you? I am sorry for you, then. As for me, I am determined to fight for what I want."

Rob was not certain he admired her motives, but he could not deny the logic of her plan. Pershing would go on as he was, destroying himself with every vice set before him, while Eloise pursued her scholarly dreams not bothered by his debauched style of living. They would never have to see each other again after their wedding.

A match made in heaven.

And since Pershing was actually well connected, Eloise's siblings would also gain the advantage of a tie to that powerful family.

What would Fiona say to this surprising turn of events?

"I hope you succeed," he said sincerely. "But I will also offer a word of caution."

Eloise winced. "Not you, too. I hear this daily from my family."

"Then you shall hear it from me as well, because it is important. Do not get caught up in the challenge or the importance of defying your family's wishes. You may live to regret your choice once you win and have your way."

"My grandmother often gave me the same lecture before she

passed on," she said, casting him a wry smile. "I assure you, this is not a mistake I will ever make. You might understand if you are ever fortunate enough to find the true matching half to your heart."

He had found it in Fiona. No two hearts were a better fit.

"Lady Eloise, a *concept*, even one as noble as higher learning, is not the same thing. A mere concept does not have a heart, and therefore cannot qualify as a mate to yours."

"And who declared this to be a rule? Why must my matching half be a person? Why can it not be a thing?"

Rob shrugged. "A thing does not have feelings. A thing cannot cry or laugh or breathe. Nor can it be a voice of conscience."

He thought of Fiona, who was a bundle of feelings, too many of them raw at the moment. If she had a fault, it could be said that she *felt* everything too strongly.

But he loved this compassionate side to her. She was his match. It was something he felt in his bones and to the depths of his soul. No logic involved. Just *knowing* that everything was right with the world whenever she was beside him.

He wanted to be that person for Fiona, too. The one she turned to for comfort, to hold her through her tears. The one to share her joys.

"Lady Eloise, if you wish to call an end to our hunting for scavenger articles, I will not mind."

"No, let's get through this or we shall disappoint our hostess. Now that I have made my position clear, what need is there to run off? Unless...are you terribly irritated with me?"

"I am not in the least irritated."

She finally gave a genuine laugh. "Should I be insulted?"

He grinned. "I did not mean it as an insult. I just appreciate honesty whenever it is offered. It happens so rarely."

"I agree."

Now at ease with each other, they had fun finding the last items and were smiling when they returned to the terrace.

He saw Fiona standing there with a score sheet in hand and

talking to another couple who had reached her just ahead of them. She was logging their finds on the sheet, obviously having taken on the role of hostess in Cherish's absence.

Had Cherish suddenly taken ill? Was there a problem concerning the child she carried?

"Is everything all right?" he asked, immediately approaching Fiona.

She nodded. "Yes, all's well. Cherish just dashed off to attend to everything else planned for today. You are the second couple to return, and I see you have found all the scavenger hunt items. Congratulations."

He arched an eyebrow.

Eloise politely thanked Fiona.

"There are refreshments waiting for you on the tables set up in the corner," Fiona said, eyeing him with curiosity.

Of course, she wanted to know his thoughts on Eloise. He would give her an earful when they had a moment alone.

"Grab yourselves a shady spot while waiting for the others," she said, still staring at him.

Rob escorted Eloise to one of the tables currently in the shade. "Care for a lemonade? Tea? Something a little stronger?"

She shook her head. "I'm fine. Lady Shoreham keeps looking our way."

"Does she? I hadn't noticed." But of course he had. His hope was that Fiona felt the mistake in giving him up to someone else, the entire impossibility of their being happy with anyone other than each other.

"She must be curious to see how we are getting along," Eloise remarked.

"Yes, I suppose."

"Ah, but there's Pershing. He seems to be wandering down the wrong path again." She nibbled her lip a moment. "Would you mind terribly if I went after him?"

Rob laughed lightly. "Not at all. Have at him."

In truth, Pershing might do well under the management of a

strong-willed wife like Eloise. She may not want him in her bed or indeed anywhere near her. But she was going to protect him even from a distance in order to maintain the benefits of her marital status.

And Pershing was sorely in need of a protector.

"Thank you. Wish me luck," she said, and scampered off.

Rob poured himself a lemonade, needing the refresher as the afternoon wore on and the wind began to die down. He studied Fiona, curious to see her expression when she realized Eloise was chasing after that drunken sot.

This was another thing he adored about Fiona, how open she was. One had only to look at her eyes or the purse of her pretty lips to know what she was thinking. No wiles. No schemes… Well, only well-intentioned schemes of a romantic nature meant to bring about a happy result. She would never plot anything malicious.

Her eyes widened and her mouth gaped open as she watched Eloise and Pershing. Then, with a shake of her head, she turned to look at him.

He smiled at her and shrugged.

She seemed utterly confused.

He drank the last of his lemonade and marched over to her. "A problem, Fiona?"

Gad, she looked so lovely with that big-eyed, befuddled stare. "Why is Lady Eloise with Pershing and not you?"

He could not suppress a chuckle. "Do not blame me. I did my duty, but it turns out she wants a useless waste of a husband like Pershing."

"What? How is that possible? Has she taken complete leave of her senses?"

"There is an odd logic to her choice. She wants a husband that she can ignore and yet still control at will."

"Rob! That is awful."

He shrugged again. "Yes, I think so. But it suits her goals. She wants to be left alone to indulge in her scholarly pursuits. Is this not why you chose this brainy bluestocking for me? Except you did not question her hard enough, or you would have learned she doesn't really want to be a wife or ever be a mother."

Pain shone in Fiona's eyes. "She doesn't want children?"

"No, love," he said gently.

She let out a ragged breath. "I see. I am so sorry, Rob. I should have been more careful in my selection for you."

"No, you did your best and chose sincerely for me. The point is, there are never any guarantees in life. Three out of those four were respectable choices, but still were not right for me. The only obvious mistake was Anne. Who chose her?"

"Cherish did."

"I thought so. She's far too trusting, but you would have seen through Anne's manipulations immediately. I expect you chose the others."

She nodded.

"Yes, they are smart, engaging, and pleasant enough look-ing...but not suitable for me."

"But Florence—"

"No, Aubrey wants her." Well, not quite true. Aubrey wanted to find out what Florence was really up to with her bird-watching stunt. And was Aubrey not the best one to discover her true purpose when he understood about birds and could easily tell if she were spinning fables?

"Then Millicent—"

"Cannot wait to leave England and explore ancient civiliza-tions. She intends to travel the world. I need to remain in England and take care of the Durham estate holdings."

Fiona huffed. "Eloise? Surely she could not *possibly* choose—"

"Do you really expect me to keep her in consideration when she has openly stated she prefers Pershing to me? To pursue her would make me a laughingstock, especially if I did lose her to that churl. Spare me, Fiona. She is out of the question."

She regarded him with utter dejection. "So, what now?"

"Nothing. I enjoy this house party and spend these next few

days with you. We are going to be teammates anyway. Cherish will send Bromleigh to sleep in the stables if he dares foist Pershing on you again. Since he loves her to pieces, he has already surrendered and offered to add me to your team."

"He hasn't said anything to me yet."

"He will," Rob said. "He understands what he needs to do to make his wife happy."

"But then you will be spending all your time with me, and this is the last thing you ought to be doing."

"Fine, I'll go riding with Bromleigh and his fellow Silver Dukes once they all arrive. Lynton's already here, and I understand Camborne and Ramsdale are due to arrive later today. I'll play billiards and drink brandy with Reggie. I'll go fishing on my own."

Her ears perked. "I don't mind fishing."

"I know," he said, smiling as he recalled those lazy childhood summers when it was too hot for them to do much more than sit under a shade tree by the stream that flowed behind their neighboring properties and dip their poles into the swift waters, waiting for a plump fish to take the bait. "Care to join me for that? How about at dawn tomorrow?"

She let out a breath. "Yes, I would love it."

"Then I'll forgo my morning ride and we'll go fishing instead. Most of the games you and Cherish have planned won't start much before noon anyway. Ah, more scavenger hunters are returning."

Fiona nodded and then left his side to greet them and mark down the items they'd found. Rob remained seated, feeling quite satisfied with how the day had turned out.

Now there was only one concern remaining.

Milbury.

Would the man use this house party as an opportunity to woo Fiona? Would Fiona encourage it?

If so, how was Rob to put a stop to it without being made to look the villain?

✦

CHAPTER ELEVEN

"FIONA, WHY ARE you crying?" Rob asked, already feeling exasperated by the time they reached their fishing spot shortly after daybreak the following day. He had chosen to settle on a grassy patch along the stream that ran behind Northam Hall and flowed southward toward the English Channel.

It looked like a promising spot, so he'd spread out a blanket for them, since the grass was still wet with dew. He set down the fishing poles and bucket of bait beside it.

Fiona ought to have been smiling, but instead she was struggling to hold back tears. He vowed he was going to give up trying to understand the fairer sex. What had happened to overset her now? Perhaps it was the remnants of a morning mist eerily hovering over the water, the long wisps moving toward them like bony gray fingers and frightening her.

Fiona was never one to easily frighten. But he could not think of what else might provoke her sudden bout of tears.

"I am not crying," she insisted, wiping her cheek with her sleeve.

"Fine, my mistake." He baited her hook, handed her the fishing pole, and was about to take up his own when he heard her sniffle again.

He sighed. "Do you not want to fish? I'll take you back to the manor, if you prefer."

"No, it isn't that. I love fishing."

He might have believed her if she weren't still weeping while declaring it. "Then what is it, love?"

"Rob, I am so unhappy."

He knew it, and it tore him apart.

He took the fishing rod he'd just given her out of her hand, set it aside, and then drew her over to a nearby fallen tree. After settling himself on the sturdy trunk, he lifted her onto his lap and circled his arms around her.

No one was going to see them, and did he really care if someone was up early and caught them together like this?

She wrapped her arms around his neck and began talking into his chest. Talking and crying.

Well, was it not better for her to get her feelings out while they were alone and no one was around to judge her or gossip?

"I am truly happy for Margaret and Cherish. I am *thrilled* for them and could not be more excited. But what if we receive similar news from Eden and Lynton, and Camborne and Jocelyn…even Ramsdale and Ailis? Having made their love matches, they'll want to start their families next."

Yes, there would probably be a wave of new babies born this year.

"And you are afraid you will be left behind?" he ventured.

She nodded. "Is it awful of me to want this so much for myself?"

"No, it isn't awful of you," he said, stroking her hair and wishing he could do something, *anything* more to make her feel less miserable. "Everyone wishes the same for you."

"Being here with you, fishing poles in hand, sent me back to a happier time when we were young and full of dreams. We saw our futures stretched out before us and everything was possible."

He nodded, but remained silent, since she had more to say and he wanted her to get it all out and unburden herself in the hope it might provide her some relief.

"We used to go fishing together on those lazy, hot summer days. Remember, Rob?"

He nodded again and smiled. "Back then, we had resolved to conquer the world. I remember."

"Then there was that last summer together when Shoreham proposed to me and I saw my life and all its possibilities laid out before me, all that promise ready to be scooped in the cup of my hands. I was already dreaming of the children we would have. I was so sure we would have four, and I gave them all names in my head."

He remembered her chattering about it. But it was all boring nonsense to a boy of eleven who simply wanted to fish.

She sniffled again. "What is *wrong* with me? Why am I not able to—"

"Stop. We don't know that the problem was ever with you."

"But—"

"No, a few short days with me in your bed does not count. I don't even want to contemplate what Shoreham did or did not do with you in all the years of your marriage. I know he was good to you, and I am not faulting him for any of this situation. But he was not all that capable in bed, and may not…"

Gad, did he dare say it?

He sighed. "I have no idea if the two of you were doing *it* right."

This only made her cry harder.

Well done, Durham. Make her feel worse, why don't you?

"What I am trying say, rather ineptly, is…you need to give *us* more of a chance, Fiona. One week is nothing. Give us several years to see if this can work."

"Living together unmarried?"

"Do not give me that it-is-sinful look. You know I would marry you this very day if you were willing. My offer of marriage remains open and shall remain so until you are ready to accept me."

She let out a breath. "You know I cannot."

"Do not start that discussion again," he said, trying to hold back his frustration. "That choice is mine to make, not yours. The world will not stop if my title is extinguished. The lands attached to the title will revert to the Crown. But everything else I own, the mines, the mills, the ships, the funds, are mine to leave as I wish. I am going to protect those who rely on me to the best of my ability. And who is to say the Crown will not pass on the grant of title to someone else who is brave and worthy?"

He kissed the top of her head and continued in a gentler voice. "Enough, Fiona. Give me your hand in marriage. It is the only way the two of us will ever be happy. Forget about giving me another three days or another week or even another year. We need to give each other a lifetime together as husband and wife."

"You will grow to despise me once you realize we can never have children."

"I could never despise you."

"Resent me, then."

"Nor resent you, because it would be my choice and I am agreeing to this commitment with full knowledge of the risks and possibilities."

"Maybe I should give us a year to see this through," she said in a hesitant whisper. "It will be time enough for you to realize the futility of this situation."

Or time enough for her to realize they were meant to be together.

He pounced on the comment, afraid she might take it back in the next breath. "Yes, a year would be good."

Hallelujah. He'd grab whatever he could.

This was what he needed, time for her to learn to put her own desires first and cease bending over backward to accommodate what she perceived as *his* duty to the Crown and the Durham title.

Whether her aching desire for children would be fulfilled was up to the Fates. Of course he wanted children. But he wanted *their* bright-eyed offspring.

He would still love her and cleave to her no matter what the future held.

The choice was an easy one for him, since he had always been in love with her. He did not want the typical *ton* marriage his parents had entered into. Those two were happiest apart from each other. What was the point of marrying if they made each other miserable?

Also, he was proud of Fiona and refused to have her appear as lesser in anyone's eyes. He would not insult her by having rumors swirl that she was his mistress. She deserved to be held in the highest regard, and that would only happen if she were his wife and duchess.

"A year seems an awfully long time," she mused as her tears abated and she began to look at him with clearer eyes.

"It will fly by too quickly," he insisted.

She sniffled yet again.

"We deserve this chance, Fiona. What have we got to lose? And we might gain everything," he reminded her, unwilling to allow her to withdraw her decision. "What is one short year out of our entire lives?"

"I know. Still, it is scary, isn't it?"

"Do you want to know what is even scarier for me? Not having you beside me in my life." He kissed her again on the top of her head. "Whatever happens, we'll work it out together."

She let out a breath and nodded. "Yes."

Blessed saints.

Had she just agreed to a full year with him? He ought to have taken her fishing sooner, for this was more than she had ever agreed to before. "Are you feeling a little better now?"

There was a note of wistfulness in her laughter. "I'm not sure. One burden removed but another added. My mind is a tangle of fear and hope. I cannot recall ever crying as much as I have this summer. But everything is changing around me and I feel helpless to stop it. On top of it all, I am a bundle of raw emotion. Those stark feelings tend to come out whenever I have my monthly courses."

As they had a few days ago, to bring an early end to their

week of debauchery. Watching her curled up in pain at the onset had left him feeling helpless. But he was glad to be there beside her, offering what little comfort he could give.

He thought back to their childhood days and remembered her very first time, for he had been there even for that. He was all of seven years old and had almost fainted on the spot upon noticing the fresh bloodstain at the back of her gown. Both of them had run screaming back to Fiona's house.

It had taken him a full week to calm down. But Fiona had chirped like a little bird and smiled throughout the week, because she was now a woman.

Perhaps this was the moment he had started to lose his best friend.

He had no intention of ever losing her again.

He raked a hand through his hair. What a history they had together.

Since she was feeling talkative, he listened to her spill her thoughts just as he used to do when they were children. Only, he never understood what she was talking about back then when she chattered about being trained to make her debut. He would simply bob his head and grunt a "yes" every once in a while as she went on about being fitted for gowns, taking dance lessons, learning how to pour tea, because friends were supposed to be interested and show they cared.

Anyway, he'd always liked the soft, lilting sound of her voice, so he did not mind her animated conversations. She was his fairy princess and even her laughter was magical and musical as it floated like tinkling crystal on a summer breeze.

"It has all suddenly become too much for me, Rob. Hearing that my friends are expecting. Seeing you with the young ladies Cherish and I selected for you. I did not think it would be so hard for me to see you with another lady."

"But it was?"

She nodded. "Brutal, in fact. All these things piled on relentlessly and made me miserable because there is the one big problem that all the wishing in the world cannot fix, the one reason keeping us apart."

"Fiona, it is the reason you *think* ought to keep us apart. But we don't even know for certain it is you who cannot have children. The point is, it does not matter to me. My heart doesn't care. My heart just wants to be with you."

"As mine so desperately wishes to be with you." She looked up at him. "Maybe it is important for me to give you that year, time for the inevitable disappointment to sink in."

Disappointment?

Honestly, why was she tormenting herself again? When was she going to understand that he was committed to loving her? To accepting her no matter the circumstances?

Had Shoreham made her feel as though she alone was at fault? Had she silently endured almost twenty years of accusations?

In truth, her husband had never come across as resentful and seemed genuinely fond of her. However, it could be that Shoreham hid his disappointment well in front of others. Or that Fiona had shoved the entire burden onto herself and Shoreham simply never stepped up to take any of the responsibility on his shoulders.

Rob shook out of his thoughts because he was going to go mad running around in circles like a dog chasing his own tail.

Fiona's spirits appeared to rise as they resumed fishing. The mist soon evaporated and the sun shone upon the water, spreading its golden aura.

They each caught a fish, but Fiona insisted on tossing them back in. "Cherish has feasts prepared for us for every meal. We'll never eat these fish, so why not let them go free?"

He tossed them back into the water.

As the day began to warm and brighten, they returned to Northam Hall. Several guests were already down to breakfast, so he and Fiona joined them.

Aubrey settled in the chair beside his. "Morning, Durham."

"You look like you've been up all night. What happened?"

Aubrey glanced around furtively, then leaned forward and whispered, "I think Florence is a spy. Did you notice she disappeared after supper last night?"

"No, I hadn't." All Rob's attention had been on Fiona during supper, during the evening games, and during Cherish's piano recital. "Where did she go?"

"I followed her as far as Milbury Hill and then lost sight of her as darkness fell. But I don't think she went much beyond that property because she only returned a few minutes behind me, after which she spent about an hour playing cards, and then retired to her bedchamber."

"Sounds like that would have been well after midnight," Rob remarked. "Maybe around one o'clock?"

Aubrey nodded.

"But you look as though you haven't slept a wink."

"Because I haven't. I kept watch on her bedchamber."

"How?"

Aubrey cleared his throat. "I might have hidden myself in the garden and positioned myself for a view into her windows."

"What?"

"I happened to have my own binoculars at hand."

"You *spied* on her in her bedchamber?" Rob did not know whether to be outraged or pity the man, since Aubrey had obviously lost all reason.

"I looked away when she undressed! What sort of knave do you take me for? I'm no Peeping Tom. This is about solving a mystery, not debauchery."

"Did you learn anything from your nighttime adventure?"

Aubrey shook his head. "Not a thing. Now I'm exhausted. I'll grab a few hours' sleep this afternoon. Milbury and his sister are to join us for supper this evening. I plan to watch what goes on between the marquess and Florence."

"Good idea. Stay close to Milbury. I'm sure he deserves closer watching."

Aubrey nodded. "You think so?"

"Oh, yes." Perhaps it was wicked of Rob to lead Aubrey amiss. But where was the harm in keeping Milbury too occupied to make a move on Fiona? That sister of his was already jealous of her and likely to arrive spewing venom.

No one knew he had spent the week with Fiona, but they would after this evening. Was this not precisely the gossip someone like Lady Cordelia would spread with malicious glee? Fiona did not need more theatrics from that wasp.

Well, he would worry about this later. No point in allowing his concerns to spoil his day, or Fiona's.

He glanced at her as she chatted with Millicent over a cup of tea, seeming more cheered now. Sometimes it helped to unload one's feelings on a person to be trusted. He was that person for Fiona.

As for Milbury's sister, she was never to be trusted. What biblical plagues would she bring down on Fiona next? Though one could always hope that Milbury would attend without her.

Fiona looked back at him, but said nothing. However, when Millicent rose to serve herself from the salvers, Fiona took the opportunity to edge closer and speak to him. "Stop looking so worried, Rob. I am not fragile."

Yes, she was. Perhaps not usually, but certainly at this moment. She seemed to be at a crossroads in her life, finding herself suddenly alone and facing an empty future unless she changed paths.

The question was, which path would she decide to take?

There were three, as far as he could tell. The first was never to marry and live out her life as a widow alone.

That would never happen. Fiona loved to be active and have people around her. She was not about to wither away in an isolated bedchamber.

The second path was to marry someone like Milbury, a man with children she could mother. But it would never be a love match because her heart was his and always had been his, just as his had always belonged to her. This would not change even if she married another.

The third was to marry him, an easy and obvious choice if only she would stop thinking of *his* duty and start thinking of their happiness.

"I had to get those tears out," she said with a sigh, "but I am much better now. Thank you for always being such a good listener…and a dear friend."

They weren't just tears. They had been shattering sobs.

Well, only a moment or two of those before she regained most of her composure. Still, it only took that moment for him to feel the punch to his own heart.

She was hurting. And he was aching for her.

"Oh, now you are scowling at me. Why, Rob?"

"I am not scowling."

"You are—I can always tell because your brow furrows and then your gaze turns hard as steel. Why?"

"Because I need to protect you."

"From what?"

He decided to be honest with her. "I am not sure how to deal with Milbury and his sister. They will be here tonight and the vile sister is going to let on that I was with you before this house party began."

"Oh, yes. I was thinking about that, too." She winced. "Lady Cordelia will make me out to be a fallen woman without scruples. I wasn't certain how to respond, whether to play into the scandal of it all, feign outrage, or look hurt and wounded for sympathy."

"How about we just let Bromleigh and Cherish know the truth?"

She gasped. "Oh, not the whole truth. Bromleigh will boil you alive."

"I only meant to let them know I arrived here early and you took me in."

"Yes, that is best. Keep it quiet, just a friend visiting another friend. You already have everyone in a dither because of that betting book on you at White's. The *ton* will be like sharks in a blood frenzy if they ever heard you had been cavorting with me."

Not necessarily, Rob mused. The *ton* likely considered her to be a merry widow who had no interest in remarrying, and therefore was out of the running.

So why should she not take London's most eligible bachelor into her bed? No commitments. No obligations.

This was why no one had wagered on her as a potential bride for him. Of course, everyone also knew she had already rejected him.

"That blasted betting book," he said. "I forgot about it...or tried to forget. I had better bring that up with Bromleigh and Reggie, too. It is your reputation that will be tarnished, and I cannot allow this to happen."

"Yes, talk to my idiot cousin and Reggie, but include his Silver Duke friends now that the last of them has arrived. They are the ones who started this wagering nonsense and should be held responsible if it turns into a mess."

"All right, but I'm fairly certain Ramsdale stayed out of their schemes. He wasn't happy when they opened a betting book on him. In truth, he was furious."

"Then he shall be a good ally for you," Fiona remarked. "Just take care of the men and I'll talk to Cherish and the other wives. Best we nip any potential scandal in the bud. They'll cover for us, the men especially. They'll feel guilty about being the ones to foist the *ton*'s attention on you and inadvertently hurting me."

"As long as they agree to fix any damage caused to *you*," Rob insisted.

"Oh, they will. Their wives will see to it that they do. They'll make their smug husbands grovel at my feet," she said with a smirk. "Rob, why don't you care about the damage to yourself?"

He arched an eyebrow. "What damage? Dukes are impervious. Nor have I ever cared what those in Society think of me. Protecting you is all that matters."

"It will be easily enough done if our friends and family just shrug off Cordelia's accusations. All they have to do is not look surprised, possibly mention they knew you had arrived early and spent a few days with me before this house party began. Innocent. Platonic. This would dampen the gossip before it ever amounted to anything."

"Possibly."

The *ton* thrived on secrets revealed, but any scandal would die before it ever had a chance to arise if there was nothing lurid lurking in the darkest recesses.

However, what would happen in the coming year when it became clear he was sleeping with Fiona? Neither Bromleigh nor Reggie would ever stand for this, but that was a problem to be addressed afterward.

Anyway, what could they do? Put a shotgun to his head and force him to marry Fiona? She was the one who needed the prodding, not him.

Fiona poked him. "You are getting too deep in your thoughts again, Rob."

He smiled. "I know."

He relented for the moment and participated in the late after-noon lawn games Cherish and Fiona had devised for the guests. As promised, he was placed on Fiona's team while Pershing was handed over to Lady Eloise's.

Rob watched as the sot was pointed in the right direction and stumbled over to his teammates. Gad, the man was a walking disaster.

Eloise looked quite pleased, however.

Fiona was also pleased, because Rob had been added to her team. They had always been an unbeatable pair.

They won their game of badminton, defeating Florence and Aubrey to take first place in a match that was breathtakingly close from start to finish. They had gathered quite a crowd by the time it ended, everyone gasping with each point made. But Rob knew the victory would be theirs, for Fiona was tenacious and never gave up.

If only conceiving a child worked this way, too.

If only Fiona's yearning could make a difference.

Their prize was a bracelet charm in the shape of a racket for Fiona and cuff links also shaped like rackets for him.

After the match, Rob took Bromleigh and Reggie aside. "Something I need to tell you before tonight's dinner party."

Fiona did the same with Cherish and Margaret. He hoped she would fare better than he expected for himself.

Bromleigh led him and Reggie into his study that happened to be unoccupied at the moment, since it was still too early for the men to be sitting around drinking. Pershing might have been found in here, but Eloise now had him firmly by the collar and kept him otherwise occupied. "What's wrong, Durham?" Bromleigh asked.

"Nothing really wrong, but I need to tell you something."

They settled in the soft leather chairs around the hearth, but Rob leaned forward, his manner stiff because he was concerned about their response when they learned he'd already been here before the house party started.

He told them, half waiting for Bromleigh's blow-up.

"The point is, I finished my business in Devonshire a few days earlier than expected. Rather than return to London and have to immediately turn around and head south again, I went to Fiona's home."

Neither Bromleigh nor Reggie appeared put out, no doubt because they never considered he was more than a guest at Shoreham Manor.

That was good.

After all, Rob may have been best friends with Reggie, but he was Fiona's friend first. This was how he had met Reggie back when they were both young boys. Later, he had been asked by Fiona to keep an eye out for the lad when they were at school together, since he was an upperclassman and Reggie was just starting his studies. He had protected Reggie from the school bullies and made a lifelong friend in the process.

"I mention it because you are about to meet Milbury's sister, and she is a miserable piece of work," Rob said.

"And Milbury?" Bromleigh asked, eyebrow raised.

"He seems to be a good sort. A widower who cannot handle his sons. They are curious boys and always up to something. The sister arrived recently to help out Milbury. I think she is just another headache he must now deal with. I cannot imagine his sons liking her at all."

"And what has this to do with you or Fiona?"

"We happened to be on the beach together, having a picnic, when we spotted his sons on a boat in the water. They were heading into trouble."

Reggie eyed him with concern. "Did they get hurt?"

Rob nodded. "One of them did, badly cutting up his leg on some jagged rocks moments before we were able to reach them. However, we rescued them, tended to the boy, and then notified Milbury. He was quite grateful, of course, and invited us to dine with him and his family. His sister took one look at Fiona and became jealous. You know how your cousin has a way of charming everyone."

Bromleigh grinned. "Yes, she has that ability. Camborne and Lynton adore her."

"Well, she charmed Milbury, too."

"And the sister felt threatened?" Reggie asked.

Rob nodded. "More than threatened. She behaved like a cornered animal and began hurling venomous accusations at Fiona."

"What did she do? Or say?" Bromleigh frowned, because as eldest cousin among the family, he felt it was his responsibility to protect Fiona.

Never mind that he had sought revenge earlier and purposely meant to rile her by putting Pershing on her team. That was merely playful retribution for the misery Fiona had put him through last year during her own house party. This Milbury situation was serious.

Rob cleared his throat. "She hurled some biblical quotations at us, mostly at Fiona. 'Harlot of Babylon' and the like. Accusing her of wanton behavior…with me. She's going to hurl those same accusations and try to humiliate Fiona when she and Milbury join us tonight. This needs to be stopped."

"What should we do?" Reggie asked, clenching his jaw in determination.

"All that is necessary is for no one to respond with surprise when she makes her accusations. If everyone claims they were aware I was here, that there was nothing untoward with my visiting Fiona, then there is no shock value."

Bromleigh furrowed his brow. "And you think this will be enough to thwart Lady Cordelia?"

"I hope so."

"May I tell Margaret? She'll be Fiona's staunchest supporter." Reggie rose, having heard more than enough and obviously eager to do whatever necessary to protect her.

"Fiona has already gone to tell Cherish and Margaret."

"Good," Bromleigh muttered. "I think we need to tell Camborne and Jocelyn, Lynton and Eden, as well. Ramsdale and Ailis, too. That ought to be a sturdy enough wall of protection for Fiona."

Rob nodded. "Yes, I was going to ask you to gather them next."

"I'll summon those Silver Dukes now," Reggie said.

"Gad," Bromleigh muttered, "stop referring to us as that."

Reggie cast him a wry look. "Oh, now you do not like it? After all those years of playing it up and making legends of yourselves?"

Rob laughed. "Admit it, Bromleigh. You, Lynton, and Camborne played it to the hilt. Ramsdale was the only one who never did, but his protestations were useless because he was an unmarried duke and had that dash of silver in his hair. The ladies were going to chase after him relentlessly once you three were taken."

Reggie nodded in agreement.

"But I am past it now and happily settled with my wife," Bromleigh insisted. "So are Lynton and Camborne happily settled with theirs. Ramsdale, too. Go on, Reggie. Bring them here."

Bromleigh watched his nephew take off, and then turned to Rob once the door had shut behind him. "Now, let us get to the heart of the matter...why did you really come early to Fiona's? And what were the sleeping arrangements?"

CHAPTER TWELVE

FIONA WAS NOT certain how the ladies would respond to finding out Rob had spent a week in her home before this house party began. Would they chide her? Be disappointed in her behavior?

What she did not expect was their cheering her on. "What?"

"Hurrah!" Cherish said, hopping out of her seat and leading the round of "bravos" and cries of "well done."

They had gathered in Cherish's private salon with Margaret, Eden, Jocelyn, and Ailis, all of them now grinning at Fiona.

"But he's a *younger* man," Fiona sputtered.

"Who is obviously interested in you," Eden said with an approving nod, and the others once again joined in. "Three cheers for you! That horrid betting book our husbands set up has put all eyes on him. They are calling him the next Silver Duke, even though he is ten years younger than the others."

"Yes, *very* young," Fiona muttered. "He is barely above thir-ty."

"Thirty-two, to be precise," Cherish remarked. "But who cares when he looks devilishly commanding and authoritative? He's a born leader."

"He is also quite handsome," Margaret added. "And he does have that lovely dash of silver in his hair. Who wouldn't adore those tiny threads among the gold? Not to mention, he is also a duke."

The others nodded.

"Everyone is betting he will choose some silly, fresh young thing just out in Society," Jocelyn said.

Fiona shook her head. "But should he not be seeking exactly this in a wife?"

Jocelyn frowned at her. "Absolutely not. The man clearly adores you, so what are you waiting for? Grab him up before some scheming ninny gets her claws into him."

This had *not* been her aim in gathering them in Cherish's salon. She'd merely wanted to let them know Rob had spent a few days with her before the party started. What they did together during that time was no one's business, but she did not appear to have fooled anyone when claiming it was all innocent.

Her blush completely gave her away. "I have no intention of grabbing him up. How can I marry him when the problem he and I face is obvious?"

"What problem?" Ailis asked.

Cherish and Margaret edged closer to Fiona, now realizing what she was about to tell the others. "I cannot have children," she said, releasing a ragged breath. "I cannot have them, and yet this is what is essential to carry on the Durham line. There are no other male heirs. Rob is the last of them. He needs sons, and this is something I can never give him."

"Does he know your situation?" Eden asked.

Fiona nodded.

"And yet he still wishes to marry you?" Jocelyn asked. "Then you have been honest with him and he is fully aware of the consequences."

Fiona shifted uncomfortably. "Yes, but this does not alter the fact that his line will extinguish upon his death if he does not sire legitimate offspring."

"Even our royal lines have died out and England has survived," Ailis remarked. "If the extinction of the Durham dukedom does not concern him, then why are *you* so troubled by it?"

Jocelyn hastily agreed. "I learned the hard way about marrying the wrong man...*almost* marrying the wretched cur. Fortunately, I came to my senses and fled the church before we exchanged vows. How foolish I looked, penniless and lost. But this is how I met Camborne. Despite his horribly rakish reputation, everything immediately felt right with him. I knew he was the one I was meant to love and marry."

"Durham reminds me a little of my husband," Ailis ventured. "Both of them are serious men who are not rakish at all. I think a man like this loves once and only. He loves faithfully and forever. If he has chosen you, then why are you so determined to deprive him?"

But would love not fade when faced with disappointment?

This was Fiona's greatest worry, that Rob would start to have regrets as the years passed and he did not have children.

"We have gotten a little off the topic," she said, clearing her throat. "It isn't about the betting book, although all eyes are on Durham because of it. Nor is it about his affection for me. It is about cutting off Lady Cordelia before any scandal can spread."

"Durham would feel honor bound to marry you if ever that happened," Margaret pointed out. "He would insist on it, for certain."

"That would put all of London in a frenzy," Ailis muttered. "I wonder what odds they have on your winning his heart? Jonas's brother made a fortune off that betting book they opened on Jonas because no one else ever bothered to learn more about him. They just assumed he would marry one of last year's crop of diamonds and wagered on ladies who were obviously never going to be suitable for him."

"No odds on me," Fiona muttered. "I doubt I am even considered in the running, since rumors are swirling that I have already rejected him. I'm sure everyone considers me too old, anyway."

"Only a fool would ever rule you out," Cherish said, raising her teacup in tribute to her. "Here's to your success! All women of a certain age shall support you, I am certain. Three cheers for maturity."

Fiona laughed. "I am impatient, outspoken, and definitely more childish than I ought to be."

"All the better," Cherish replied. "Durham has always been remarkably mature for his age. Even as a young man, he showed wisdom well beyond his years. Hooray to those of us considered on the shelf…and to the men clever enough to choose us." She turned to Margaret, who was the youngest among them by several years. "Do forgive me—I do not mean to disparage your youth and vigor."

Margaret, who was the sweetest among them, although Ailis was a close second, smiled back at her. "Oh, Cherish. No offense taken. I am cheering just as fiercely as you are. Love must always triumph. Isn't it wonderful that he cares so deeply for you, Fiona?"

Yes, it was.

But did Fiona dare reach for this temptation of happiness?

She hugged them all now that her mission had been accomplished. Cordelia's malicious insinuations would be addressed if and when the time came. As for the possibility of her ever marrying Rob? She had agreed to give him a year. Fate and her wishes for a miracle would determine what happened next.

"Then we are of one mind? If Lady Cordelia casts any aspersions, you are all to simply feign boredom."

Eden grinned. "Oh, yes. We shall yawn and dismiss any possible spark between you and that gorgeous man."

Fiona headed back to her bedchamber to prepare for this evening's dinner party, hoping her friends would not let her down. She was surprised by how supportive they had been about Rob, none of them considering him a mismatch for her.

In truth, this did cheer her.

"Take that, you miserable wasp," she muttered, ready to swat the spiteful Cordelia if she dared to cause harm.

Also of concern were Bromleigh and Reggie, who considered her under their protection, since they were her closest male kin.

Would they take the news of Rob's visiting her as well as their wives had?

She had almost made it to the safety of her guest bedchamber when the pair walked up to her. "Fiona, come with me," Bromleigh said, his voice deep and laden with ducal authority. Reggie also had a serious expression on his face.

"Go away, Gawain. You too, Reggie. I will not be lectured to by either of you," she said, tipping her chin up in defiance. "What did Durham tell you?"

"Everything," Bromleigh responded.

No, Rob was too discreet ever to do such a thing.

"Where is he now? What have you done with him?"

Bromleigh cleared his throat. "I have asked him to leave."

"What?" This genuinely surprised Fiona. After all, Rob had been friends with all of them for many years, and a good and loyal one at that.

"He'll join us for supper tonight, but has agreed to leave at first light tomorrow morning. I will not have him—"

"Ruin me? What am I, some sixteen-year-old ingenue? Good grief, I was married for almost twenty years. And who are you to dare pass moral judgment when it took you over forty years to get around to doing your duty, and your own behavior was reprehensible in the meanwhile?"

"It is not the same thing," he attempted to argue, but she cut him off with an indignant gasp.

"I cannot *believe* you would do such a thing to him! Or ever believe Durham would use me ill! No one treats me with more respect than he does. If he leaves, then I will leave. And you can explain *that* to Cherish and Margaret."

She shoved both of them into her bedchamber and shut the door behind them because she was not finished excoriating them yet. "Of all the stupid, preposterous ideas you have ever had, Gawain! How can you think Rob was ever anything less than a gentleman? More of a gentleman than you ever were. Need I remind you of your reputation before you married Cherish? It was *appalling*. And then you were so stupid as to try to match Reggie with Cherish when all along you loved her but were too stubborn to admit it! And you think to control my life? My choices?"

She hardly drew a breath before continuing. "And you, Reggie."

He held up his hands. "What did I do?"

"You are going along with Gawain's foolishness. I'll see you both sleeping in the stable with the horses," she muttered, and then left them gaping at her while she walked out of her bedchamber to find Rob.

"Of all the gall," she grumbled, marching down the hall to knock at his door.

After knocking louder when no one responded, she simply barged in. He wasn't there, so she searched for him downstairs.

She grew worried when she did not find him in the house or garden or stable, but his carriage was still in the carriage house, so he could not have left yet.

She finally spotted him standing beside the stream where they had been fishing at daybreak this morning. "*You*," she said, striding forward to confront him, too. "What did you tell Gawain?"

He arched an eyebrow and regarded her with obvious confusion. "What are you talking about?"

"He told me that he had banished you as of tomorrow. Is this true?"

Rob nodded.

Fiona felt her heart tighten, as though someone had caught it in a vise and was now squeezing hard. Rob was the kindest, most thoughtful man alive. It shamed her to think he was being treated so badly because of her. But had he said something that ought to have been left unsaid?

"Why would Bromleigh do such a thing unless you confided our private business to him?"

His eyes widened. "Do you seriously believe I would ever be

so indiscreet? But I did tell him that I arrived early to propose to you because I am in love with you."

She groaned. Of course. Rob was so infuriatingly noble sometimes. "Why did you tell him that?"

"Because it is the truth. I love you and marrying you has always been my intention. I did not come to you for the chance of bedding you for a few days…as enjoyable as satiating myself on your body was. I hoped to prove we belonged together for a lifetime."

"But you never said a word to him about doing…*you know*…with me?"

"Of course not."

She shook her head, now thoroughly addled. "And he kicked you out because of your honorable intentions? How could he be so cruel? What else did you tell him? You must have said something more."

"No, Fiona. I said not a word," he insisted, frowning in that lovely, serious way he'd done ever since he was a little boy, and she had grown to love. "That love fest you and I had going on is no one's business but ours. Nor would I ever say anything to embarrass or shame you. Surely you know this."

She let out a breath. "I do, Rob."

"What did you tell the ladies?"

She felt her cheeks heat. "Nothing, but I do not think I hid my feelings as well as you."

"You do not hide your feelings at all," he said with a light groan, smiling wryly as he brushed a stray curl off her cheek when the wind whipped it out of place. "So, they know you behaved like a wanton and craved me in your bed?"

She smacked him lightly on the shoulder. "Rob!"

His smile broadened. "Do you crave me, Fiona?"

"Shut up. The point is, you cannot leave. I will not allow you to leave. I've told Gawain that if you go, then I go, too."

"Why? He was not wrong in wanting to protect you."

"From you? Of all people? Hah! You are the last person on

earth who would ever hurt me." She felt indignant and at the same time anguished, because he was not blaming her, even though she was at fault for his now being treated so shabbily.

"I'm glad you think so, but you are wrong about this. I think we have it in our power to do more damage to each other than anyone else ever could. In fact, you are the only one who could ever shatter my heart because I gave it to you so long ago and you still have full possession of it. I need you to hold on to it, Fiona. Hold it and cherish it as I will always cherish yours. This is why Bromleigh wants me gone. Can you blame him? My presence is only causing you a mountain of pain, and he does not want to see you hurt worse than you already are."

Her eyes began to water. "And he thinks kicking you out will somehow make it easier for me?"

He sighed. "Are you crying again?"

"No… Maybe! Having you with me these past few days has made this the most wonderful time of my life. I will not have it end before I am ready."

"Let's be honest with each other, shall we?" he said, sounding more bitter than she had ever heard him. "All we are doing is digging our knives deeper into each other and leaving gaping sores. How will this end, Fiona? Will we keep cutting each other up until our hearts are nothing but shreds?"

She stared at him, hardly able to breathe. "No, being with you can never be wrong."

"Then why must we ever part?"

"Because…it is for you. Only for you. How will you feel five years from now when you realize there can never be any children for us?"

"I already know this is likely and am willing to take the risk. How many times must I say it?"

"It isn't merely likely but *certain*. Rob, you will grow to regret your choice. You'll look at me with the same wretched disappointment that Shoreham felt as the years passed and I could not give him children. I cannot bear for the same to happen with you.

Not with you. I would never recover from that."

She covered her face with her hands and quietly sobbed. "Why can you not stop loving me? It should be simple to do. Aren't I more of a nuisance than I am worth?"

"Shoreham made you feel as though you were to blame?" he said with more than a trace of anger in his voice. He took her hands in his and moved them off her face so she could not avoid looking at him. "Why did you not tell me sooner? Is this what has been torturing you all along? Oh, love. What happened? Why would he do this cruel thing to you?"

She released a pained breath. "He was not trying to be cruel, but he was certain I was the one at fault. You see, there was an incident in his younger days. A lady claimed she was with child and he was the father. It happened several years before he and I met and married. I never learned of it until well into our marriage."

"This is why he blamed you? Since he had supposedly fathered a child, the lack had to be entirely yours?"

She nodded. "When he confessed this to me, I suggested we find them and help them out because Shoreham... Well, I am ashamed to say that he paid the woman a small sum of money to keep her quiet about this embarrassment, and then forever afterward ignored his responsibility to her and the child."

"Assuming he had any duty to them at all and it wasn't simply a ruse on the part of the lady in question," Rob said, his voice low, as though he were quietly contemplating this revelation and feeling considerable outrage on her behalf. "Shoreham wasn't exactly the brightest candle when it came to women. He could easily have been duped by someone with a scheming nature."

"I considered this possibility. However, we shall never know. She got the money out of him months before the child was born, before she was even showing, or so he claimed when I got the details out of him. He never saw her after that or ever bothered to find out whether she had given birth and whether it was a boy or a girl."

"It was a child born out of wedlock, so I doubt it mattered to him," Rob mused. "And the lady never came back to him asking for more?"

Fiona let out a ragged breath. "No, she never did. I quietly started a search for her."

"Why? Were you thinking to delight Shoreham with a son he never knew? Obviously he did not care, or he would have conducted a search himself."

"I don't know why I did it," she said miserably. "Feelings of guilt for my failing, perhaps. In any event, I wanted to make certain the child, if he or she were ever found, would be properly cared for. Shoreham never knew and I never told him anything of what I was doing. The Bow Street Runner I hired to investigate the matter was reputed to be one of the best. A man by the name of Homer Barrow."

"I know of him," Rob said, still holding on to her hands and gently stroking them with his thumbs because this was his nature, always determined to comfort and protect her. "He is very good at what he does."

"Several months later, he gave me his report."

"What did he tell you?"

She struggled not to cry again. "He claimed there was a child."

Rob's eyes widened in surprise. "And he is certain it was Shoreham's?"

"Well…"

"What, Fiona? What are you not telling me? Was there a doubt about the paternity?" He began to quietly seethe. He'd always had this way about him, a quiet strength that made one feel secure when confiding in him.

She nodded. "Some questions, yes. Mr. Barrow reported to me that the young lady married a young man shortly after receiving Shoreham's money. The pair sailed to Boston within a month of the wedding. He found out very little more, for her parents had passed away by the time I engaged Mr. Barrow to investigate. So had the young man's parents. He could find no siblings or other family members to question, so he sought information from neighbors and friends. Some had heard she had given birth to a child, but that it did not survive past infancy. A girl, one of the neighbors told him."

"Yet you say Mr. Barrow had doubts? Did he believe her approaching Shoreham was a ruse? That she had duped him into believing the child was his in order to give her funds enough to cross the Atlantic and start a new life with this young man?"

Fiona let out a shaky breath. "He thought it was a possibility, but could not say for certain. He had no proof, only a gut feeling."

Rob pursed his lips while in thought. "So, after all this, you still remained in doubt."

"No, Rob. This was confirmation that the fault was mine. The girl came from a respectable family, a local tradesman's daughter. She was not some transient woman off the streets. Does it not make sense that a father, upon learning of her situation, would quietly find a good man to marry her and take her away in order to avoid scandal?"

"Or perhaps this man was her sweetheart all along and they devised this scheme in order to amass enough funds to start a new life. Did Mr. Barrow dig up information on this young lady's character? Or that of the young man? What of her family life? Was the father strict? Cruel? Your Bow Street man must have sensed something amiss to claim he had doubts even if he had no hard proof."

"There was nothing more to dig up," she replied in anguish. "The family had a good reputation and so did the young lady. But she and the man she married have also died. We will never know the truth now. Are you willing to risk the future of a dukedom on her being a liar? A tradesman is a man with roots to a place and one who holds respect in his village. Does it not seem more likely she was telling Shoreham the truth and her father was desperate to fix the situation before others noticed her waddling around with a belly the size of a house? All the more reason to find her a husband and have them sail away before too many questions were asked, especially if that child was going to arrive early."

Her heart tightened and she struggled to contain another bout of tears. "I don't know which is worse, Shoreham's being duped or that a child he had sired did exist and we will never know what truly happened to the poor thing."

"No, the worst is Shoreham's choosing to believe he had fathered a child in order to put the full blame of a childless marriage on *you*. That wasn't fair of him. Do you think he was the sort to ignore a child he was convinced was his?"

Heat shot into her cheeks, for her answer was embarrassing. "Yes. He was good in many ways, always very proper and respectable, but this mistake was something he wished desperately to ignore and forget."

"And yet he did not ignore it when it served to conveniently place all the fault on you for a childless marriage. I would never do such a cowardly thing to you." He raised her hands to his lips and kissed them, then leaned forward and kissed her softly on the lips.

She groaned as she felt the warm press of his mouth on hers, wishing she had the strength to pull away. But she never would, not with him. "You must never tell anyone about this, Rob. Please, I need your promise."

"Upon my oath, this stays between us," he said sincerely, and kissed her again with more ardor and a measure of protective fierceness.

"Nor should we ever speak of love or hearts or of the hope of forever between us," she said once her lips were free of his.

He regarded her with surprise. "Are you still belaboring this issue? Thinking to sacrifice our happiness for my supposed good? Based upon what you think Shoreham might have done? Fine, then I'll raise a glass in toast to one year with you. This is what you've agreed to, and I mean to hold you to it. An entire year to spend in your bed, getting on you, *in* you, and under you, and into any other position you will allow, only to be kicked out at the end of that time because of your wrongheaded conclusion that you cannot give me the son I need to preserve the Durham title."

"It isn't wrongheaded."

"Yes, it is. Completely and utterly. All the more inane because of what you have just told me about Shoreham. Why are you still placing full blame on yourself?"

"Rob, why won't you see reason?"

"Why won't *you*?" he shot back.

"He had a child with another woman! Just because Mr. Barrow had a feeling something was not right, does not make it so. The evidence points to Shoreham having had that liaison that led to the birth of a child. *His* child."

"And this is why you will throw away our happiness? On a maybe that the blame had to be all yours? Or is this the way you really want it? Me in your bed but no commitments. Then forget our year together. I will not fight you on this any longer. I'll stay through the dinner party, protect you from Lady Cordelia's barbs, but then I will leave as Bromleigh asked of me."

She inhaled sharply. "And wait for me at Shoreham Manor?"

"No," he replied, raking a hand through his hair. "I am going to leave you forever because there is no getting through to you, is there? You are using anything and everything as an excuse to keep us apart, purposely making a mountain out of the *insignificant* difference in our ages and your belief that you are barren."

"Being childless is not insignificant."

"If Mr. Barrow's gut instinct tells him Shoreham might have been duped, then I am with him. I am truly sorry the proof is not clearer. Intensely sorry for all the anguish it has caused you. But I am fully aware of the risks and am willing to take them. Why aren't you? What are you so afraid of, Fiona?"

"Rob..." She paled, although she had no reason to feel despondent when she had been the one to push him away this entire time. If he left now, would she ever see him again? "Rob..."

"No, Fiona. Don't do this to me."

"Do you think this is any easier for *me?*"

He took her in his arms and gave her cheek a light caress. "I know it is awful for you. Horrid. Painful. Heartbreaking, because you still have doubts about yourself. But I don't and never have. You have only to say yes to my offer of marriage and I will be yours forever. This is all I have ever wanted. Stop making up rules for us. Stop choosing my wife for me. I know who I want, and it has always been you."

She could no longer contain her feelings, and they burst out in a sob. "The ladies said I was an idiot not to marry you."

He arched an eyebrow. "Are you going to prove them right?"

She laughed amid her wealth of tears. "Rob…"

"Fiona, enough. I cannot bear it any longer. Truly, this situation between us is ripping me apart. Forget adding another day, another week, or another year. Stop doubting. Stop trying to manage everything. Stop trying to control what is impossible to control. Just trust in our love. Do not be afraid. Whether we are childless or have ten children, you won't ever lose me. So end my agony and say you will marry me."

She looked up at him, staring into his gorgeous, silver-flecked eyes. "Gawain had no right to treat me like a child. If I wanted you in my bed, who was he to object? No one has the right to tell me what to do. Nor do they have the right to order you to keep away from me. If I want to be with you for a night, two nights, or even a lifetime, that is for me to decide."

"Do you want to be with me for a lifetime?"

"You know I do. I want this more than anything."

"Then no one can ever stop us from being together. Only *you* have this power. What are you going to do? No more dithering. Make your decision now, Fiona."

She felt so torn inside, her heart completely shredded. But she understood that she would lose him forever in this very moment unless…

She let out several shaky breaths. "If I want to marry you,

then I will, and no one is going to stop me."

His eyes widened and he smiled. "What are you saying?"

"I don't know." She had spent her entire adult life shouldering the blame for something that might not have been her fault, although she sincerely believed Shoreham had fathered a child. Even if he had, who was to say their inability to have children was all on her?

Rob was not Shoreham. He would always love and protect her. He was everything to her.

Which scared her all the more, for he was the last person she ever wished to disappoint.

"Look at me, Fiona. *Trust* me. Take that leap. Think with your heart and not with the *ton*'s false notions of duty to a title that should never have been mine. Will you accept my proposal?"

She hugged him with all her might. "Dear heaven, Rob. I am so frightened."

"Don't be, love. I have you. I will always have you and hold you, love and protect you, for as long as there is breath in me. This is our destiny, Fiona. Don't fight it. This is how we were always meant to be. Just say you will."

She continued hugging him, and now her eyes were squeezed shut tight. She couldn't breathe. Not even her heart dared beat.

"I will, Rob. Yes. I will marry you," she said in a ragged whisper. "I love you so much."

"Yes?"

She laughed and looked up at him. "Yes."

He lifted her in his arms and whooped with glee. "She said yes!" He shouted it into the wind while twirling her in his arms. "Yes, yes! She's going to marry me!"

She did not stop him from cheering or shouting it to the heavens, although no one was ever going to hear him at this distance and above the noise of the swiftly moving current of the stream.

"I love you, Fiona," he said, heartily laughing with the relief of it.

"I love you to the moon and back, Rob." An enormous weight suddenly lifted off her, too.

She felt freer than she had ever dared hope, free and elated even knowing the impossible problem they faced, one he seemed certain would never destroy their love. She was not as confident yet, for it was a problem that would hover over them like an ominous cloud throughout their marriage.

She reminded herself again that Rob wasn't Shoreham. He would never foist all the blame on her. He was her protector, and would protect her even from his own disappointment as the years dragged on and she remained barren.

If only she could give him everything he wanted.

No, that wasn't quite right. He *wanted* her, and this he had. What he *needed* was a son to carry on the Durham line.

She doused the glimmer of hope that it might happen. She dared not think it was possible.

Nor was it a need he felt as acutely as she did. Perhaps in time he would come to regret it, but right now he looked happy…his dream come true.

Indeed, he looked ridiculously gorgeous as he smiled at her with a brilliance that outshone the sun.

The air surrounding them felt deliciously warm and light.

Together.

They would work through the good times and bad together.

She stared up at him. His smile had never been broader, a big, sloppy smile that stretched from ear to ear. His soul-deep eyes had never looked more sparkling, for he was obviously filled with joy.

Perhaps he understood better than she ever had that their bond was forged in iron and unbreakable. He must have felt this ever since he was a little boy. Even then, he'd been so handsome and serious, looking up at her with worshipful eyes.

"We should make the announcement tonight and marry before this house party ends," he said, never one to waste time in gaining his objective. "Cherish and Margaret will attend to all that needs to be done in time for the wedding breakfast. Not to mention, this will shut up Lady Cordelia for good."

"Oh, she'll still find something venomous to say about us."

"Who cares? You'll be my wife and…although I know it is not proper *ton*, for most dukes and duchesses maintain their separate quarters, do you have any objections to our sharing a bed?"

She found his wicked grin impossibly appealing. "Rob, are we really going to do this?"

"Share a bed? Behave wantonly and do the nasty deed?"

She laughed. "I am speaking of our getting married."

He nodded. "Is tomorrow too soon for a wedding?"

CHAPTER THIRTEEN

ROB HELD FIONA'S hand as they walked back to Northam Hall, afraid to let go of her lest she fly away on a gust of wind. He dared not breathe or glance at her for fear she would change her mind. But holding her hand anchored her to him and made this moment feel real.

She had agreed to become his wife.

He had never felt such joy arising from a moment of despair, for only a short while ago he had been standing alone at their fishing spot watching his hopes be carried away in the stream's fast-moving current. In that moment, he had given up on his dream of ever marrying her, certain he had lost Fiona forever.

Then suddenly, there she was beside him, her chin wobbling as she held back tears.

He saw into her heart, saw how badly it was tattered and torn to pieces because she loved him so fully, with all her heart and soul, and yet felt herself unworthy to be his wife.

Her? *Unworthy?* She was his fairy princess and would always be this magical sprite for him.

Even now, her dark, windswept curls danced about her ears and her eyes shimmered as bright as starlight.

In truth, Bromleigh had not ordered him to leave so much as begged him to do the right thing and stop giving Fiona so much pain. "She's barren, Rob. That ache remains with her day in and day out. Do you think it is easy for her to refuse you? She does it out of love for you, knowing a wife who can bear you sons is what you need."

Yes, he did need sons.

Yes, he hoped for children.

But if it meant losing Fiona in order to have them, then the choice was an easy one for him.

He would always choose Fiona.

He meant to seek out Bromleigh and thank him for giving her the push she obviously needed to give up her obsession with salvaging the Durham line. There had been a few intelligent but ruthless Durham dukes who had built it into one of the most powerful titles in England. However, for generations there had been mostly wastrels and fools.

A few had been beheaded. A few had lost the title only to reclaim it when their faction rose to power again.

Most of the recent Durham men had died before ever ascending to the title because they were reckless idiots who'd managed to destroy themselves before they ever got their hands on the dukedom's assets.

Rob had never been raised to be a duke. In truth, he was either forgotten by his father or beaten whenever in that ogre's company.

He wasn't sure which was worse.

His mother had gone along with it all because it suited her life of luxury, and she had no wish to disrupt the convenient arrangement reached between her and his father. For this reason, she'd easily convinced herself that beating strength into him, watching that brute beat a helpless little boy, was all right.

So, did he care about the Durham title?

Not nearly as much as he cared about Fiona, the fairy princess who had nursed his wounds and held his hand throughout his pain, and, with that gesture, lessened it.

And now she would be his. Because it was his turn to lessen her pain.

He dared not blink and lose it all.

Since Bromleigh and Cherish were busy getting ready for their dinner party, he and Fiona chose not to disturb them now and agreed to take them aside just before the meal commenced. The general announcement would be made later in the evening, once the men had imbibed their ports and joined the ladies in the parlor.

Of course, Rob had every intention of speaking up during their meal if Lady Cordelia said anything out of line. "All right, Fiona? If she spouts her venom, I am going to announce our betrothal there and then."

"All right. Agreed."

He breathed a sigh of relief. She was not going to back out.

He escorted her back to the house and they parted ways at the top of the stairs, he turning left to his guest chamber while she turned right to head to hers.

He entered his room with a smile on his face, and kept that smile as he undressed and then washed up.

He saw his reflection grinning back at him as he adjusted the tie of his formal black attire with the assistance of Gawain's valet, who was making it his life's mission to see it knotted to perfection.

He then endured more fussing as the man measured the distance between his cuffs and sleeves to ensure just the right amount of white lawn shirt was showing under his jacket sleeve. The world would not collapse if too much of the white lawn was showing, but Rob dared not say this to the earnest man. So he smiled and thanked him.

In truth, he had never felt better.

He strode downstairs and marched into the parlor where the guests were to gather before being led into the dining room for tonight's feast. Fiona was there, chatting with several other guests. He recognized Aubrey, Florence Newton, Milbury and his waspish sister, Lady Cordelia, and the other wasp at this house party, Lady Anne Hastings, all of them standing in a circle around Fiona as they conversed.

He felt a moment's concern upon noticing that unpleasant pair, Cordelia and Anne, standing together.

Evil seeks out evil.

He did not like that they were both beside Fiona, and worried they would destroy her confidence with their insidious comments. It had taken a huge leap for her to overcome her guilt about being childless and agree to marry him.

His fears were allayed when she lit up like a bright candle the moment she saw him standing at the threshold and motioned him over.

Perhaps he was the one blazing like a fully lit chandelier and brightening the room. He did not know, and he was too elated to care.

Her smile meant everything to him.

He approached and bowed low over her hand. "Lady Shoreham, you are looking particularly lovely tonight."

Well, Fiona always looked beautiful in his eyes, but even more so tonight. She wore a gown of dove-gray silk, a strand of small pearls threaded through her upswept hair.

"So are you, Durham," she said with a merry lilt of laughter.

Aubrey and Milbury grinned at him.

Lady Cordelia and Lady Anne looked upon him with grim smiles that spoke of their insincerity.

Ah, what a pair of jackals.

After Rob had greeted the ladies and gentlemen within Fiona's circle, Milbury drew him aside. "Durham, I would appreciate a moment of your time. May we speak with candor?"

Rob arched an eyebrow, but agreed. The two of them stepped onto the terrace.

He did not like the idea of being apart from Fiona even a moment this evening, but she was quite capable of standing on her own and would resent his behaving like a protective ape.

Besides, she did not look worried. Knowing her, if those two wasps dared to insult her, she would swat them down with elegant efficiency.

She could be vulnerable with him because she trusted him. But with those two? She would be fierce as a tigress.

"What is it you would like to know, Milbury?" he asked, enjoying the light breeze that swirled around them as they stood in the outdoor twilight and spoke in private.

"What is the extent of your feelings toward Lady Shoreham? I mean, it is obvious you care a good deal for each other, but…" Milbury raked a hand through his hair. "You see, my boys are quite fond of her too. I was thinking to court her. I had a very happy marriage and a good home life. My wife was cheerful and compassionate, and I see my boys are missing this joy in their lives very much. My sister is never going to replace this. In fact, I need to get her out of my home as soon as possible."

Rob suppressed a groan, for that was quite the understatement. His sister was a vindictive menace, and her presence in his household would do more harm than good for Milbury's sons.

Fortunately, it appeared the marquess realized it and meant to address the problem. "I do not want to get between the two of you if there is something more serious than…er, friendship. It seems as though there is. Am I reading this wrong, Durham?"

Rob did not want to confide his newly betrothed status to Milbury just yet, but did have to say something to alert the man. "I would suggest someone other than Lady Shoreham. She is wonderful in every way, but her heart is taken."

"By you?" Milbury cast Rob a wry smile. "Are congratulations in order?"

Rob let out a breath. "I hope so."

"Well then," Milbury said with a little disappointment, "what of these other lovely ladies? Would you recommend any of them to me? Truthfully, they all seem too young. They are closer in age to my sons."

"I'll ask Lady Shoreham on your behalf, or you could ask her yourself. She has a wide circle of friends, and no one can be better trusted with the task of finding a worthy lady for you and your sons. She prides herself on being an excellent matchmaker."

"Then I will take a moment and ask her. Thank you, Durham." Milbury shook his head and gave a wistful laugh. "I enjoyed being married. I think I was very fortunate in the choice I made, even though I was a young idiot in my twenties who thought of himself as quite the rake. How was a man to choose only one lady to share his life when there were so many lovely ones flitting about him like glittering butterflies? And then one evening I saw my Jessica standing beside a potted fern, actually trying to hide behind it because she was so shy and felt over-whelmed at her first ball."

Rob smiled and let Milbury go on speaking, for it seemed the man had held his grief in for a while and was only now trying to come out of it.

"I was quite expert in going about in Society, for I had attended more than a dozen balls already. We exchanged glances from across the room. That was it. Everyone and everything simply melted away. The orchestra, the dancers, the footmen dashing about with trays in hand—all suddenly vanished, and all I saw was my Jessica. Then and there, I knew I was going to marry her. There would be no other lady for me." He sighed and shook his head again. "But my sons need a good and loving lady to take on the role of mother, so I must think of them and do what is right. This means taking the plunge and marrying again."

As the dinner bell sounded to draw the guests into the dining room, Rob realized he and Fiona had not spoken to Bromleigh and his wife to break their good news.

Ah well. Fiona may have said something to them on her own.

But she gave a light shake of her head to advise him that she had said nothing.

He thought to have a quiet word with Bromleigh during their meal, but he was not seated close enough to him or his wife. To his dismay, he found himself placed between Lady Anne and Lady Cordelia.

Seriously? Was Bromleigh determined to torture him?

He glanced at Fiona in dismay.

She cast him the sweetest, most sympathetic smile, and it lightened his heart. He no longer minded that he had been given the worst dinner partners ever devised in the history of such parties. Well, he wasn't thrilled about it, but he could endure anything knowing Fiona was close by and committed to their marrying.

In truth, they knew each other so well, they often seemed able to communicate with a mere glance. But his feelings were in too much turmoil for him to be certain about any silent signals they exchanged tonight.

Had he made a mistake in encouraging Milbury to confide in Fiona? The marquess truly seemed a decent and honorable fellow. Nevertheless, Rob felt a pang of uncertainty when he saw that Milbury had been seated beside Fiona. Well, Florence Newton, the fake bird watcher—if Aubrey was to be believed— was seated on the opposite side of Milbury. He would figure out a way to get Florence chatting with Milbury if it looked like he were getting too cozy with Fiona.

If that didn't work, Rob would somehow catch Reggie's eye and get him to distract Fiona, for she was seated beside Milbury to her right and Reggie to her left.

He wanted to give Milbury the chance to ask Fiona about her circle of London friends, ladies who were in their thirties, either widowed or spinsters who might be suitable for this lord who was feeling quite lovelorn at the moment.

But was it not prudent to also make certain Milbury was not going to change his mind and go after Fiona?

The sad truth was, Rob did not trust that she was all in on her decision to marry him. Her feelings remained too fragile. She had resisted for so long.

Perhaps he ought to stand up now and blurt out the simple words. *Lady Shoreham and I are betrothed.*

That would end all speculation. *And* close that stupid betting book at White's. Not to mention put an end to Lady Anne and Lady Cordelia's ability to demolish Fiona's confidence.

He shook out of his thoughts as he heard Lady Cordelia mutter, "That harlot is all over my brother."

Fiona and Milbury had their heads bent slightly toward each other as they spoke. They were hardly "all over each other," as Cordelia was accusing.

But Lady Anne had heard the comment and bared her teeth in a malicious smile. "I've heard rumors about her wanton behavior. I hear she has had several lovers," she said, looking directly at Rob. "Seems she has now set her cap for Lord Milbury…and you may find yourself in need of consolation."

Was Anne offering her services?

To remove any doubt, she discreetly ran her hand along his thigh. "I am available."

Rob squelched the knot of disgust forming in his stomach. He did not know whether to ignore Lady Anne or toss her a look that warned he was not amused.

Upon brief consideration, he decided to ignore her, for would it not give her more fodder if she saw that he reacted?

Lady Cordelia leaned forward to stare across him as she addressed Anne. "I will *never* allow that woman to sink her claws into my brother."

Lady Anne laughed. "Surely he cannot care about her. She's too old and dried up to be seriously considered, even for a man of his age."

"My brother can be foolish about such things," Cordelia replied. "But I intend to put a stop to her."

The hair on the back of Rob's neck began to prickle. What did that evil witch have in mind?

He immediately drew back his chair, stood up, and raised his glass of wine. "A toast to our host and hostess."

"Hear, hear!" several guests said, also raising their glasses.

Rob cast Fiona a pained stare.

Did she understand what he needed to do?

She smiled and rose, also raising a glass to the Bromleighs. "A toast to my cousin and his lovely wife…and to the Duke of

Durham, a trusted friend since childhood, and now more than a friend. May we tell them, Durham?"

He nodded. "Please do."

"I'll let you make the announcement," she said, no doubt noting his distress and wanting him to say whatever he felt needed to be said.

At her urging, he proceeded. "Lady Shoreham has agreed to become my wife. I am elated to announce we are now betrothed."

Those around the table erupted in cheers.

All but the two miserable ladies seated beside him.

He understood Lady Anne's bitterness, for she had come to this summer house party to snare him. However, Lady Cordelia should have been pleased to learn Fiona was no longer a threat to her standing within the Milbury household.

But no. The woman was as miserable and dour as ever, her lips pursed and body stiff. However, it was the looks she continued to cast Fiona that had him worried.

Did she simply resent anyone's good fortune? Or was her jealousy particularly fixed on Fiona, who was as lovely and beloved as Cordelia was bitter and alone?

After the meal, everyone moved onto the terrace to watch the sun set over the water.

The waspish pair must have been hovering in wait for just the right moment when his back was turned to make their move and approach Fiona. Rob noticed the pair sidling toward her as he finished a conversation with friends at the opposite end of the terrace, and was about to return to Fiona's side when they caught his eye.

Fiona was speaking to other guests, unaware and engaged in lively conversation while standing beside the balustrade. Everyone was looking upward, distracted by the evening's display, for the sunset was a particularly magnificent blaze of reds and yellows tonight.

Rob had been standing with several of the Silver Dukes on

the opposite end of the terrace, accepting their congratulations on taking the leap to marriage, when he noticed those two suddenly position themselves on either side of Fiona. "Excuse me," he said, his heart beating faster as he made his way through the crowd toward her.

He did not have far to go, merely the length of the terrace. However, impeding his movements were the distracted onlookers *oohing* and *aahing* at the sky, and Bromleigh's footmen, who were circulating among the guests carrying trays laden with champagne glasses to hand out for Bromleigh's formal toast in honor of Rob and Fiona's betrothal.

Rob's breath caught in his throat when he saw the pair nod to each other and place their hands to the small of Fiona's back.

Did they mean to push her off the terrace?

Fiona was standing up front with Margaret and Cherish, her hands on the stone balustrade as she marveled at the sunset. None of them were paying attention to those two jackals.

He was only halfway through the crowd when Margaret suddenly noticed what was happening and must have given Anne a sharp elbow to the ribs, because the woman suddenly doubled over. In the next moment, Cordelia let out a cry as Fiona also realized what was happening and dodged out of the way at the same moment the shrew attempted to shove her.

Unable to stop herself, the wretched harpy found herself pushing air, lost her balance, and tumbled over the balustrade into the bushes below. "My ankle!" she screamed amid the gasps and cries of others who had seen her topple off the terrace, which was raised a little higher off the ground on that side. The fall would not have been deadly, but still precipitous enough to cause injury.

Cherish, Margaret, and Fiona held Anne on the ground while several gentlemen rushed down the steps to reach Cordelia.

Too bad that witch had merely broken an ankle, Rob thought. This was no doubt what she had hoped to do to Fiona—have her break a limb because she could not bear to allow any happiness to go unpunished.

"Fiona! Are you hurt?" He found himself trembling as he took her into his embrace.

"I'm fine, Rob. Truly." She hugged him back, but quickly eased out of his arms to return to assisting her friends in holding down Anne, who was still struggling and now attempting to kick her way free.

Oh, gad. These ladies were with child.

Rob took over, urging Margaret and Cherish to back away while he drew Anne to her feet. However, he kept a firm grip on her arm as he called for her parents to attend him in Bromleigh's study.

But he did not notice them in the crowd, and no one seemed to know where they had suddenly disappeared.

Rob called over Potter, Northam Hall's ever-efficient head butler. "Will you please find Lord and Lady Hastings and deliver them to the study? Once there, do not leave them unattended. I will arrive shortly to speak to them."

"At once, Your Grace," Potter said, and ordered two footmen to follow him.

Aubrey came over to take hold of Anne, leaving Rob free to see to Fiona.

She nestled in his arms. "Wasn't Margaret splendid? And Cherish, too?"

He nodded, wanting to laugh at the sight of the three of them subduing Anne while Cordelia was toppling into the garden below. He would have found it hilarious were it not for the possibility they might have been hurt themselves. He wasn't going to calm down for a while after witnessing that close call.

Reggie and Bromleigh pushed their way through the crowd to reach their wives, their faces ashen when they realized what had just happened.

"Cherish, dear heaven! What were you thinking?" Bromleigh growled as he drew his wife into his arms and let out a shuddering breath.

Cherish frowned up at her husband when he released her. "I was thinking to help my best friend. Would you not have done the same?"

"Of course, but...but..." He glanced helplessly at his wife, no doubt wanting to chide her for risking her own safety while in her delicate condition, but could not say anything, since they had not made the formal announcement yet.

"Besides," Cherish said, her manner softening as she noticed her husband's dismay, "I merely helped to hold her down after the fact. It was Margaret who laid her low."

"My sweet Margaret?" Reggie's eyes widened as he wrapped an arm around his wife's waist. "What did you do?"

Margaret regarded him with big, innocent eyes. "I merely applied what you taught me."

Bromleigh stared at his nephew. "Reggie, what in blazes have you been teaching your wife?"

"How to defend herself," Reggie said with a ring of pride. "I wanted her to be able to protect herself if ever I was not around. I'm so proud of you, love. But...what happened?"

Margaret quickly explained. "You know how you can just *feel* malice in a person?"

Rob supposed it was that same uncanny ability that made the hair on the back of his neck prickle whenever he sensed danger.

"I noticed what she and Cordelia were about to do, so I..." She showed her husband her exact motions, although she did not use any force when digging into his ribs with her elbow.

"Well done," Reggie muttered, and kissed her on the cheek.

"How did Cordelia take a tumble?" Bromleigh asked, staring at Fiona. "Weren't you the one meant to go over into the bushes?"

Fiona cleared her throat as she nodded. "I knew to dart out of the way upon hearing Margaret's warning, so she missed me, and...well, she might have tripped over my foot."

"You tripped her?" Reggie asked.

Fiona looked marvelously indignant as she tipped her chin up.

"My foot was there. How is it my fault she stumbled over it?"

Rob let out a breath and whispered in her ear, "Thank goodness for your big feet."

She laughed and swatted his shoulder. "That remark is going to cost you."

He grinned, knowing he could tease her in this manner because she actually had dainty feet, and she knew he adored everything about her.

But the incident had given him a scare, and they all needed a little humor injected to relieve the tension. Finding himself in need of more relief, he kissed Fiona more thoroughly than he ought to have done.

But when would he get away with kissing her in public like this again? After all, they had just announced their betrothal and had been about to celebrate with a champagne toast before those two crones had attempted to harm Fiona.

The betrothal toast was postponed for twenty minutes while he and Bromleigh first dealt with Anne and her parents. They were appalled, ashamed, so disappointed in their daughter, and apologized profusely. They offered to pack up and leave this very night, but Bromleigh took pity on them. "First thing in the morning will do. There are too many dangers in traveling in the dark."

They next met with Milbury, who attended them without his sister, since she required medical treatment for her broken ankle. Ramsdale, because of his experiences on the field of battle, was able to attend to it without need to summon a doctor.

Cordelia ought to have been grateful, for she would have been left writhing in pain for hours were it not for his capable treatment.

But gratitude was not in her nature.

Milbury appeared quite humiliated as he joined him and Bromleigh in the study. "Durham...Bromleigh... I don't know what to say. I am horrified by what my sister attempted to do to Lady Shoreham. Obviously, she is not well. I ought to have noticed it sooner, but I was so lost in my own grief, I... Well, that is no excuse. Thank goodness she managed to harm only herself. But I shudder to think what she might have done to my boys if they ever displeased her."

"Yes, get her away from them immediately," Rob said.

"This very night," Milbury agreed, and then gave an agonized groan. "To think, I considered having her look after them. I expect you shall want me to leave now and want nothing more to do with me or my family, who have caused you so much trouble. I fully understand and will not blame you."

Fiona had come in to join them and heard most of what Milbury said. "Your sister is the one who must answer for herself. I do not blame you, Lord Milbury."

He turned to Fiona, not realizing she had been standing at the threshold and listening in. "But I am responsible. I should have been more alert and noticed her behavior had become erratic. She'd seemed a bit withdrawn since coming to Milbury Hill, but I attributed it to fatigue from her travels. Dear heaven, for this reason I had not pressed her to take over the care of my sons."

"Who has been watching them?" Fiona asked.

He winced. "I have. They've been in my care these past few days...my incompetent care. But she was meant to take over the task starting tomorrow. Thank goodness I delayed it. The idea of having her watch my sons? No, it is all my fault."

Fiona frowned. "Why are you placing all the blame on yourself? You are a good father who was trying to do right by his children."

"And might have exposed them to great danger," he said with a wealth of feeling to mark his continued anguish. "Lady Shoreham, I shall understand if you refuse to ever speak to me again or ever have anything to do with me or my boys."

"Nonsense. You are all welcome at Shoreham Manor, as I hope Durham and I shall be welcome at Milbury Hill."

"Most assuredly," he said with much surprise. "Both of you have an open invitation. I cannot begin to thank you for all you have done for my family."

"But you will understand if your sister shall never be permitted to set foot on my property," Fiona added.

Milbury let out a breath. "Nor will I allow her anywhere near mine again. First thing in the morning, I shall be making arrangements to place her in a sanitarium, where she may live out the rest of her days in comfort but under watchful care. In the meantime, I shall have to figure out how to be enough of a father to those lads to make up for the loss of their mother."

"You'll do fine, Milbury," Fiona said. "But call upon Durham and myself if ever you are in need of assistance."

Milbury rose and bowed over her hand. "I will try my best not to abuse your kindness, Lady Shoreham. Nor will I allow my boys to trouble you very much. It may not be easy, for they regard you as their fairy princess."

Rob smiled at Fiona when she glanced at him. Yes, she was *his* fairy princess. Soon, his wife. He could not fault Milbury's sons for having good taste.

Bromleigh spoke up once Milbury left. "Fiona, are you all right?" It was just the three of them now.

"Yes, perfectly fine thanks to your wife and Margaret."

He released a deflated breath. "I'm so sorry your joyful moment was ruined. Shall we try another toast to celebrate your betrothal?"

She nodded. "Yes, have your footmen pour everyone another glass of champagne. But give me a moment alone with Rob. There is something I need to say to him."

Rob's heart hitched. Was she backing out?

No, she would not have agreed to another toast.

Bromleigh left them in his study and shut the door behind him to allow them privacy.

"What is it, love?" Rob asked when she stood before him and simply stared at him.

"I was so afraid."

He took her into his arms. "When? Out there on the terrace

when Anne and Cordelia—"

"No, not that. Even if they had managed to push me over, I would have ignored any bruises or broken bones and gotten up out of spite to unleash my fury on them. You know I am no meek flower."

He smiled, for she could indeed be fierce when she wanted to be. "You would have had them cowering."

But she could also be soft and vulnerable, as she often was with him. And now, for her to admit she was afraid meant something serious.

"What scared you, Fiona?"

"These past few years," she said, still looking up at him, "as my love for you changed from abiding friendship into something more… I did not think it possible for you to love me as much as I loved you. I did not realize love could bury itself so deeply into one's soul or devour one's heart so completely."

He cast her a wry smile. "It was always this way for me and my feelings for you, holding you in innocent love when we were children, and then it blossomed into something more."

"I felt the same," she said. "It has taken me until now to accept this is real and trust in our feelings."

He shook his head. "What you mean is that you did not trust mine."

"Only because I dared not believe you could feel this way about me, too."

He frowned. "Was it not obvious? Have I not made an idiot of myself over you?"

She smiled. "I couldn't see it because the depth of my love for you frightened me so much that it blinded me in many ways. I made up all these excuses about why I should not marry you. I was too old. I could not give you children. I could never—"

"We don't know that children are out of the question."

"Oh, Rob," she said, her smile fading. "Do not get your hopes up for something that will never happen."

"And do not be so certain it won't. But if it turns out you are right, I will never be disappointed. Whatever my future holds, it will be a future with you in it. With *us* together, as we were always meant to be. I found my fairy princess when I was barely a lad out of leading strings—she just took a little longer to find me."

"Rob…"

"Yes, love?"

"Do you think it is possible for us to marry tomorrow?"

✦

Chapter Fourteen

THE DOOR TO Rob's guest chamber opened as Gawain's valet entered to assist him in preparing for his wedding day. It had taken only two days to get everything in order, allowing the ceremony to take place on the morning of this third day, which was filled with sunshine, soft white clouds, a gentle breeze, and the bluest sky.

All was moving along smoothly until Rob heard Fiona's shrieks resounding through the halls of Northam Hall, where they were all still staying, since the house party had yet to draw to a close.

"What the...?" He tore out of his bedchamber and raced to hers.

"Your Grace! You are not dressed!" the valet cried, running after him.

Perhaps not fashionably dressed, but Rob had on his trousers and shirt, although the shirt was not buttoned. Fortunately, his trousers were. And what did the state of his attire matter when Fiona was in danger?

He reached her bedchamber slightly ahead of Gawain, Reggie, and several other guests. Her door was open and she was seated beside her vanity, her little derriere perched on the vanity's stool.

She looked quite lovely, wearing only her robe, which hugged her every delightful curve, and her hair was in a riotous tumble down her back.

Cherish's maid stood in the center of the room, wringing her hands. "I don't know what's wrong, Your Grace."

Rob nodded and looked around the room. Nothing appeared amiss.

His heart was still in his throat as he strode forward and knelt beside Fiona. "What in blazes has you so overset?"

"Can you believe it?" she wailed, holding up her hand.

He had to peer closely to notice the lone strand of hair snared in her fingers.

A mouse hair?

A rat hair?

"No! It's mine!" she exclaimed when he dared mention those rodents.

Rob scratched his head. "Yours? So what?"

"Look!"

He was staring at it and still had no idea what she was talking about.

"Can you not see? It is a *gray* hair!" She closed her eyes and sobbed again. "It isn't even a pretty silver color, just drab, and how soon before my entire head is covered in gray and I look like an old charwoman?"

"You are never going to look old or like a charwoman," he said, relieved the issue was not Milbury's deranged sister escaping and coming after Fiona. "You will always look beautiful to me."

"You're just saying that because you love me."

He laughed. "How is that a bad thing?"

She allowed him to wipe the tears off her cheeks with his thumbs. "It is awful because you are so young and fit. I would not mind nearly so much if you were dumpy and had warts. But just look at you. There is no one handsomer."

He had rushed in with his shirt undone, and she was now staring at him and muttering something about his perfect chest and rippling muscles.

"Is this in any way fair, Rob? Your hair is freshly washed, too, and…" She traced a finger along his skin, following the trail of droplets sliding down his neck, onto his shoulders and chest.

"It's my wedding day. I thought I would wash up for my blushing bride," he said with a grin.

Fiona brushed away the last of her tears and laughed. "Your deranged bride, is more like it."

"No, she's my fairy princess," he said in a whisper, then turned to the others. "No cause for alarm. Merely a mad countess on the loose."

Reggie rolled his eyes and then took charge of dispersing the crowd. "Rob, can I leave you to deal with Fiona? I have my own problems."

"What's wrong, Reg?" Rob asked.

"Nothing serious. Margaret's stomach is in upheaval. I've left her moaning on the bed with her face over the chamber pot. She might have eaten something that did not agree with her."

Did Reggie not realize yet Margaret was carrying his child? Hadn't she told him?

Well, that was not Rob's concern at the moment.

He knelt beside Fiona. "You do realize that was a completely insane and hysterical response to finding *one* gray hair on your head? I already have a dozen, and you do not find me shrieking and blubbering about it."

"Because you are perfect and have an old soul that makes you wise and sensible instead of mindlessly hysterical like me," she said, now cracking a genuine smile. "It caught me by surprise and I handled it poorly. But I am approaching forty and…they'll call me the Silver Duchess."

"First of all, you appear nowhere near forty yet. You look beautiful and magical, just as you have always done and will always appear in my eyes. No one would ever guess you were above the age of twenty. You have a very young face."

She laughed again. "It is a good thing your eyesight leaves much to be desired. But I like that you see me through the eyes of love."

"Always, Fiona."

She nodded. "I know."

"Ready to get married?"

"Yes." She cast him one of her captivating smiles that reached her eyes and made them sparkle. "If you will still have this deranged countess."

"Never a doubt. Come on, get dressed or we shall both be late to our own wedding."

Rob finished dressing and headed downstairs to join his friends in the entry hall while awaiting the ladies. The house party guests had all been invited to join them at the local parish church for the ceremony, after which they would all return to Northam Hall for the wedding breakfast Cherish had organized with the assistance of Margaret and the wives of the other Silver Dukes.

Reggie appeared particularly bemused as he stood among the men.

Rob frowned as he walked over to his friend. "What's wrong? Is Margaret still feeling ill?"

Reggie let out a breath and raked a hand through his hair. "Yes, but she still insists on attending the wedding and claims it is nothing of concern."

Rob arched an eyebrow, uncertain whether to give his friend a hint. Reggie looked so perplexed that he decided to take pity on his friend and give him a slight prodding. "How long has this been going on?"

"Oh, about two weeks now. Mostly mornings, and then she's suddenly fine and back to her beautiful self."

"Are you finding her particularly beautiful lately?"

"Of course, because I love her more each day. What are you suggesting?" Reggie paused a moment and stared at Rob.

"Gad, are you that dense? Has she been *glowing* lately?"

"Yes, now that you mention it. A lovely glow about her. I…" He inhaled sharply. "Rob, I have to go!" He tore up the stairs.

Rob watched him, smiling.

"What's with Reggie?" Bromleigh asked, coming to his side.

"He's checking on Margaret."

Bromleigh grinned. "You've figured it out, haven't you?"

"Figured what out?"

"Margaret's condition. I spotted it immediately, since this is what Cherish has been going through. Was that Reggie just catching on?"

Rob chuckled. "Yes. A happy day all around."

But Bromleigh frowned. "How will Fiona take the news?"

"She knows already," Rob said, letting out a heavy breath. "Margaret confided in her when she first arrived at your house party."

"Oh, blast. Then she's been aching this entire time?"

"She's happy for her friends, genuinely delighted. You know she hasn't a malicious bone in her body. She would never resent their good fortune."

Bromleigh nodded. "Still, it has to be hard on her."

"It is," Rob said quietly. "But she'll have me now, and I hope that will be enough for her."

"It will. I'm glad she's marrying you." Bromleigh gave him a friendly clap on the back. "You've always understood her better than anyone else. And love goes a long way toward healing wounds, doesn't it? This is what she deserves, a true love match."

All conversation ceased once the ladies came downstairs.

Fiona looked stunning in a gown of blue silk that flattered her youthful figure. Her hair was drawn back in soft waves and fashioned in an intricate chignon at the nape of her neck. The simple style seemed to enhance the graceful beauty of her face.

She wore no diamonds or other sparkling gemstones, only the lapis lazuli necklace and ring Rob purchased for her on their day in Brighton. She must have chosen this particular gown because it was the exact color of that ancient stone and held significance for both of them.

He still had the chunk of stone he'd purchased as an after-thought. It was buried amid his undergarments in his bureau drawer.

He had no idea what he would do with it. Perhaps it was enough to be in his possession, quietly bringing him good fortune wherever it was needed.

Their gazes locked.

Her smile stole his breath away.

She was happy.

And she loved him.

Within the hour, they were at the church and standing with the vicar before the altar.

Rob's heart pounded harder as the time drew near for their exchange of vows.

He had never felt more content or at peace as when Fiona said, "I do," and he said the same in turn.

"I now declare you to be husband and wife under the eyes of Our Lord and in his house," the vicar intoned.

Cheers resounded and belfry bells pealed as they marched out of the church.

Everyone now climbed into their carriages to ride back to Northam Hall for the wedding breakfast.

Fiona's entire staff had been invited to attend the ceremony and the breakfast that immediately followed. There was not a dry eye among them, for they truly adored her and wished her every happiness.

"We'll be returning to Shoreham Manor this evening," Fiona told her housekeeper within earshot of her staff of maids, who tried to be discreet as they ogled Rob and giggled.

Blessed saints. Were they still mooning over the sight of him shirtless?

All he cared about was Fiona finding him worthy to ogle, and he hoped she would never tire of his presence in her bed.

The day was filled with good news as Bromleigh and Cherish formally announced they were expecting a child, which prompted several other newly married couples to do the same. Reggie and Margaret, for one, although they made clear it was very early days yet. Ramsdale and Ailis also announced they were expecting their first around Christmastide.

Then Lord Barclay rose and cleared his throat. "I am delighted to announce that my daughter, Eloise, has accepted Lord Pershing's proposal and agreed to marry him."

This was met with a moment of stunned silence from the revelers before everyone finally recovered from the shock to cheer and wish them well.

Rob expected the proposal had been the other way around, Eloise ordering Pershing to marry her, and he was too deep in his cups to contradict her. "Good luck, Eloise," he muttered, for she would need quite a bit of it to keep that drunken sot in line.

However, she looked quite pleased. Pershing seemed not as drunk as usual, and not as scared as expected. In truth, he seemed not to mind terribly that he had been snared by that bluestocking.

Perhaps that mismatch might work after all.

The wedding breakfast was drawing to a close when Aubrey approached Rob. "Durham, I need a moment of your time."

It wasn't a request so much as a demand. The man appeared distressed.

"What's wrong?" Rob asked, as they melted away from the crowd and walked down the terrace steps to stroll in the garden.

"It's Florence Newton," Aubrey said, clearing his throat. "I think she is a thief."

"What?" The remark genuinely surprised Rob. "Why do you think so? Has she stolen anything from Bromleigh's guests?"

"No, not them. But I think this is why she was snooping around Milbury's home a few days ago. I have been watching her these past few nights."

"Still?" Rob groaned. "Aubrey, what in blazes are you doing?"

"Getting ready to confront a thief," Aubrey insisted. "She stole into Milbury's home the day after Lady Cordelia tried to push Fiona off the terrace. It's true, Durham. I saw her do it. She went into Milbury Hill empty handed and came out with a small pouch. I am almost certain there were jewels in it."

"Seriously? Jewels?"

He nodded.

"Have you said anything to Milbury?"

Aubrey nodded again. "I spoke to him privately later that day, never mentioning Florence. However, I asked him to check his valuables, because I told him that I noticed someone sneaking out of his house while I was out bird watching. I said that I could not make out who the person was, but he and his staff should conduct an inventory."

"Did he?"

Aubrey nodded yet again. "But he claims nothing was taken."

"Why are you still accusing Florence, then?"

"Because I know she took something from that house."

"Have you asked her what it was?"

Aubrey groaned. "I was hoping you might help me. Will you do it?"

"What? Me confront her?" Rob shook his head in disbelief. "I'm rather busy right now, or haven't you noticed it is my wedding day?"

Fiona happened to join them at that moment. No doubt she had been looking for him and wondering what he was doing away from the party. "Who are you confronting?"

"No one," Rob said. "I am not getting involved in Aubrey's nonsense."

Fiona's ears perked. "What nonsense?"

Aubrey sighed. "You may as well tell her, Durham. You're going to do it anyway, aren't you? You have that besotted, I-love-my-wife look about you, the sort that tells me you will keep no secrets from each other."

"This is what happily married couples do," Fiona explained. "But you are obviously distressed. What do you want us to do?"

He quickly told Fiona what he had seen.

Rob expected her to refuse him, but she nodded. "Fine, I'll speak to her."

Rob took her hand. "No. What if she is dangerous?"

She rolled her eyes. "Florence? Seriously? Both of you wait here. I'll bring her into the garden and then we shall all ask her what is going on. She is not a thief, for pity's sake."

She marched off and returned within a few minutes with Florence in tow.

Florence adjusted the spectacles on the bridge of her nose and stared back at them. "Fiona, why have you brought me out here? I hope you are not thinking to match me with Lord Aubrey, because I—"

"Match you with me?" Aubrey retorted with a snorting huff. "If I wanted you, then you would know it. If I kissed you, rest assured you would be melting in my arms and begging for more."

It was her turn to reply with a snort.

Aubrey frowned. "I don't need others to woo a woman on my behalf."

"Then why are we here?" Florence asked.

"I saw you take something from Lord Milbury's home," Aubrey shot back.

Florence blushed. "That's it? And now you believe I am a common criminal? Utterly lacking in moral rectitude?"

"You said it, not I," Aubrey replied with a soft growl.

Fiona stepped between them. "Florence, I know you are not a thief. Please tell us what is going on. Is Lord Milbury into shading dealings? This is something I need to know, since he is a neighbor of mine and I must protect my staff."

"No, Lord Milbury is a gentleman." Florence let out a breath and her shoulders slumped. "It is his sister who is a little magpie and likes to collect shiny objects."

"Like gems?" Rob asked.

She nodded. "She noticed Fiona's lapis lazuli ring and necklace, but she couldn't get her sticky hands on them, since Fiona always wears them. They are lovely, by the way."

Fiona smiled at her. "Thank you."

Aubrey frowned. "Whose jewelry did she steal?"

"A friend of mine's. I have been investigating the theft that occurred at my friend's house party last month and narrowed the suspects down to one, namely Lady Cordelia. I knew she had done it, but I could never find the gems. So when Jocelyn and Camborne asked me to join them here, I was happy to accept. I knew Lady Cordelia intended to move in with her brother for the long term and would have to take her belongings with her."

"You took advantage of the opportunity and searched her room?" Fiona asked.

"Yes, knowing I had to do it before she settled in and squirreled away her loot where I might never find it. As it was, she had merely tucked the pouch in one of her drawers, so I quickly found it. I assure you, Lord and Lady Wilmot will confirm everything I have said."

Rob smiled. "Well, glad that's settled."

Aubrey remained frowning. "You might have been hurt. What if she had walked in and caught you?"

She looked up at him, obviously surprised. "First of all, Milbury had taken her away that morning to settle her in a sanitarium. Even if he hadn't, do you think she could have chased after me with a broken ankle? Are you worried about me, Lord Aubrey? That is wonderfully protective of you. But rest assured, I am careful in the investigations I take on."

His jaw dropped. "You mean you've done this more than once?"

She nodded. "Yes. Oh, do not give me that apish look and start lecturing me. I am more than capable of taking care of myself."

She bade them a good day and walked off.

"Unbelievable," Aubrey muttered, and went off after her.

This left Rob alone with Fiona. "Do you still believe there could be something between them?" he asked.

She shrugged. "Time will tell."

Rob grinned. "Perhaps the Silver Dukes will open a betting book on him. After all, his father is now the Duke of Weymouth and Aubrey is next in line. He may not have a dash of silver in his hair yet, but I expect Florence will quickly turn his hair gray if he ever chooses to pursue her."

Fiona laughed as she glided into his outstretched arms. "That would be an interesting match, wouldn't it? More important, I am glad they can now close the betting book on you."

"They never should have opened it, for I was always yours." He kissed her deeply, determined to be her duke and her starlight, for this was what she always claimed to feel whenever they coupled.

Starlight.

That night, when they left the revelers and returned to the privacy of Fiona's home to share their first night as husband and wife, he carried her over the threshold and up the stairs to her bedchamber.

He kicked the door shut with his foot, not ready to set her down yet.

A lamp had been lit and left atop her bureau, casting the room in a soft, golden light. "First time for us," he said, giving her cheek a nuzzle.

She laughed gently. "Rob, you and I have done this before. Were you not the one who claimed we were rutting like rabbits?"

"Yes, but never as husband and wife." He set her down and began to undress her, for he was aching to have at her sweet body, aching to feel the softness of her skin against the hard expanse of his.

He kissed her as he untied the lacings of her gown. And kissed her some more as he drew the pins from her hair and watched the lush mane tumble like dark silk down her back.

"Let me help you," she said once he had stripped her down to her chemise.

"Not tonight, love." With a groaning laugh, he quickly undressed himself. "I am going to expire if I must wait another minute to have you under me."

Within a breathless instant, he had disrobed. He now slipped the chemise off her body so that they stood naked before each other, each of them hungrily looking their fill.

He loved the shape of her body, the fullness of her breasts, especially. But she also had a prettily rounded bottom and long, slender legs. Her dark tresses were a gloriously untamed cascade down her back, the ends curling at her hips.

He continued to look his fill as he swept her back into his arms and settled her in the center of the bed. Then he doused the lamp, for he now wanted to see her by the silvery shadows of moonlight.

And amid the glow of starlight.

She reached out her arms to him.

He settled atop her with a soft growl, careful to remain propped on his elbows, because he was big and she looked slight and delicate beneath him.

His blood turned hot and pulsed through him like the thick flow of lava.

They were husband and wife.

She was his to claim in marriage.

His to love forever.

He cupped her breast, running his thumb lightly over the rosy bud and then lowering his mouth to suckle and tease it.

Sweet. As sweet as the apples they used to pick from her family's orchard. This was her scent, apples and autumn spices.

He slid his hand down her body. She moaned and threaded her hands in his hair, tugging as she urged him to go faster.

He laughed. "Fiona, I do not want this over within a minute."

"It won't be," she assured him, her breaths now coming fast and her eyes wild and shining with passion as he breached her threshold and embedded himself inside her. "Oh. *Oh.* Don't you dare slow down. We can do this again all night. But I need you *now.*"

Hellfire. Their first time as husband and wife was going to be hot and ravenous, a molten explosion of heat and desire.

So be it.

He did not hold back.

They were soon an incendiary tangle of limbs, pure fire and volcanic eruptions as he poured himself into her and held nothing back.

Not a blessed drop would be left in him.

They tumbled over the precipice at the same moment, their damp bodies clinging to each other as the final quivers of pleasure tore through them.

He grunted like a satisfied beast and rolled onto his back with a heavy release of breath. "Gad, that was good."

She laughed and leaned over to kiss him, for she had also reached her starlight moment.

This came as no surprise to him.

He'd always felt they were one heart.

One soul.

Neither complete without the other.

He made growling panther sounds as he inhaled the warm apple scent of her skin. She purred in response. He kissed her with scorching heat.

You are mine, Fiona.

Mine forever.

When the kiss ended, she look up at him in wonder.

This intimacy was new to her, and it felt right that she had never shared this with anyone but him. Her body was hot and felt wonderfully soft as she curled like a kitten against his side.

Blessed saints. She was so beautiful, it took all his willpower not to start up again.

"Starlight," she whispered, and smiled up at him.

"Starlight," he agreed.

The windows were open and a light breeze filled the room, mingling with the hot scent of their passion.

This was how they drifted off to sleep, in sight of a canopy of stars and the silver glow of the moon.

They got little sleep, however.

Their bodies were not done with each other yet.

All it took was for one of them to softly stroke the other, and their fires blazed.

"I love you, Fiona," he whispered, watching her in an unguarded moment as the sun rose and its golden rays shone across their bed.

"Love you so much," she mumbled while asleep beside him, her lips soft and pink, and her dark hair in a wild tumble upon her pillow.

This was the best moment for him, watching her by the light of morning and knowing he had the right to share this bed with her from now on. No more sneaking away like a thief in the night.

He leaned over and kissed her on the shoulder.

She looked small and lovely beside him. Still a fairy princess.

His fairy princess.

He quietly rose and tossed on his trousers before walking over to the window to look out over the garden and the cove waters beyond. This mist was burning off water, and the gentle waves were already glistening as the sun's rays struck them.

Fiona must have felt his absence, because she now stirred. "Rob? Could you not sleep?"

He smiled. "Best sleep I've had in years, love."

She donned her nightgown, which had lain unused on their bed, and padded to his side. Holding her face up to the sun, she sighed. "It's going to be another perfect summer day."

He drew her into his arms. "A hot day. Look how strong the sunlight is upon the water already."

"No, Rob. There's no sunlight."

He arched an eyebrow in question. "No sunlight?"

"Only starlight," she said, smiling up at him. "Beautiful, sparkling starlight."

"Is that so?" he said with a light chuckle.

She nodded. "Nothing but shimmering stars."

"Then I am mistaken and it must still be nightfall. Care to join me back in bed?"

Her smile broadened. "I can be persuaded."

EPILOGUE

Shoreham Manor
Near Brighton, England
July 1819

ROB HAD EXPRESSED no objections when Fiona insisted on holding another of her summer house parties, since it had been a long-standing tradition at Shoreham Manor. Last year, she had ceded the annual party to her cousin Gawain and his wife, Cherish, because they wanted to show off their newly refurbished home, the neighboring Northam Hall.

But Fiona was eager to be back in full force as hostess.

"Sure, love," Rob had said when she first brought up the topic. "Who do you want to invite?"

"Well, I was thinking…" She had shown him a neatly written list, obviously something she had been giving thought to for weeks, possibly months.

And now their guests had begun to arrive.

Fiona was smiling broadly, glad to have reclaimed the role of hostess.

But this year's party would be more of a family affair rather than a crush of debutantes and bachelors hoping to make advantageous matches. Bromleigh and Cherish now had a newborn daughter, while Reggie and Margaret were the proud parents of a son. Ramsdale and Ailis had sent their regrets because she had just given birth to twin girls and the trip to Brighton was simply too much to undertake.

Lynton and Eden had come down with Lynton's children,

who seemed to thrive under Eden's nurturing. His sons had made fast friends with the Milbury boys, which proved a little hard for Priscilla, Lynton's youngest, for she was the only girl among them and feared she would be left out of all the fun. However, Milbury's boys turned out to be very kind lads and went out of their way to include her in all their adventures.

Eden and Lynton went along to supervise the children, because adventures usually meant trouble, and this was something they were eager to avoid.

Jocelyn and Camborne were the last to arrive at the week-long party, happily making the trip down from Scotland to be among friends. They would stay on for an entire month before returning home because it was nonsensical for them to come all the way down here just to turn around and head north again. "This might be the last trip we make in a while," Camborne announced with pride. "With the Lord's grace, we may have a little bairn before the end of the year."

"Congratulations," Rob said with hearty enthusiasm, grinning at Camborne, whose buttons were about to pop because his chest was so puffed up with pride.

Jocelyn stood smiling beside her husband. "The midwife told us it's to be a boy. I have no idea how she can tell, but she claims it is obvious by the shape of my body. If the weight gain is all up front, it is a boy, she insists. I've heard she is never wrong."

Rob spared a glance at Fiona, worried that she might be feeling some heartache now that so many of their friends had started families of their own. But she seemed fine and surprisingly at ease with all of this domesticity.

A schedule was developed, the children dining early and then being sent upstairs under the watchful eyes of two of Fiona's most trusted maids. The Milbury boys often slept over, which proved easier, since the Lynton children and Milbury boys got along famously and never tired of playing with each other. Nighttime treats were plentiful—milk and cakes, biscuits, fruit, and hardier fare if any of the children were particularly famished, which they always were.

The adults dined later on their own, and it was on a balmy summer evening with the full moon aglow that they sat around the table discussing what the *ton* was to do now that there were no more Silver Dukes on the Marriage Mart.

"But you're forgetting Lord Aubrey," Rob said. "We have kept up a correspondence. His father passed away a few months ago, and he is now a duke."

"The Duke of Weymouth," Eden added. "He's kept in touch with us, as well. Sadly, his father faded fast and left poor Trajan a bit overwhelmed. But he's a capable fellow and will handle the responsibility. He had already taken over most of the duties while his father was alive."

Lynton snorted. "He's kept in touch with *you*. We all know he's been holding a torch for you ever since you were first introduced."

"Not true," Eden insisted. "He has moved on. He never loved me. I was merely an infatuation."

Rob was not certain about that, but he hoped Eden was right.

After all, Aubrey had shown a more than passing interest in Florence Newton. Yes, that interest had been mostly because he believed her to be a thief, and this was why he had been following her around like a hound on the scent. But that misunderstanding had been cleared up, and Rob sensed something could have developed between them.

Well, what did he know? His heart had been claimed by Fiona from his earliest days, and he had never had serious feelings for anyone else.

His experience with women came from inconsequential dalliances. Sometimes a lot of dalliances, especially after he had graduated from university, entered Society, and realized Fiona was the only woman he would ever love.

But she was married to Shoreham at the time.

Lord, he'd suffered over those years.

He had never considered seducing her. She was a good person and took her marital vows seriously. Violating them, even with a man who truly loved her, would have shamed her, and she might never have gotten over that feeling of sin.

But now, she was his to love and honor.

"Aubrey?" Bromleigh muttered, rubbing his hands together in glee. "He'll be the perfect target."

"Aye," Camborne said, holding up his wine glass. "A toast to the next Silver Duke—once Lord Aubrey, and now he must get used to his new title, Duke of Weymouth."

Rob raised his glass. "Who will open the betting book on him?"

"I will, of course," Lynton said, grinning at his wife when she gave him a light poke in the ribs. "Do not maul me, Eden. I only wish to see him happy. What is so wrong with that?"

"You wish to see him happily *away* from Eden," Fiona jokingly retorted. "But it is a fine idea. I think everyone deserves to find love. I sincerely hope he meets his perfect match."

"Do you think it could be my friend, Florence?" Jocelyn asked, raising her wine glass in toast. "If bets are to be taken, then my wager is on her."

Cherish frowned. "But how will they get together? She purposely avoided him last year at my house party. I don't think she liked him all that much."

Rob exchanged a grin with Fiona.

"Aubrey will be busy running the Weymouth holdings for years to come. It is possible they will never meet again," Cherish continued with some dismay.

Margaret also had her glass raised. "They will, if they are truly destined to love each other. Love always finds a way. And I did sense something between them."

"I surely did not see it," Reggie muttered, but he cast his wife a doting glance. "However, if Margaret noticed a spark, then there's a spark. Open up that betting book as soon as you return to London, Lynton."

Lynton nodded. "Eden and I will be taking the children there as soon as we leave here."

"The thornier issue," Camborne remarked, "is how are we to get them to meet again? I doubt either one of them plans to return to London anytime soon."

"We cannot get involved," Fiona insisted. "If it is meant to be, then as Margaret said…it shall be."

Rob rose and held up his glass. "To Aubrey and Florence—may they not merely find love but crash into it headlong."

Bromleigh laughed heartily. "Hear, hear!"

They all repeated the joke and had a hardy laugh over it.

As the hour grew late, the men stayed up to play billiards and share rounds of brandy while their wives retired early.

Rob tried to be quiet as he stumbled into their bedchamber in the wee hours, but Fiona was awake. "Sorry, love. I didn't mean to make so much noise."

"You didn't," she said, slipping out of bed to assist him in undressing. She laughed as she untied his cravat and the slight tug on the fabric made him tip toward her. "Can you stand up straight?" she asked as he planted a kiss on her forehead.

"I don't think so. I keep tilting toward you. It's that magnetic attraction." He hiccuped, realizing he might have imbibed a little too much. "Do you know that you grow more beautiful with each passing day? Gad, you're *so* beautiful."

"I did not know that." She smiled and helped him out of his shirt.

"Well, you do. And you are." He kissed her on the nose. "Because you are my fairy princess and I love you."

She had him sit on the bed and helped him off with his shoes. "I love you too."

"I know." He hiccuped again. "I've never been happier. Have you?"

"Never happier, my love. I have something to tell you. I'm not sure you will believe it. I'm not sure I can believe it myself. Are you sober enough to listen? Perhaps it is best left to tomorrow."

He took gentle hold of her hand and drew her onto his lap. "I'm sober enough. What is it, love? Something troubling you?"

She let out a shaky breath. "I've been counting the months."

"Since we married?" He groaned. "Gad, have I missed our anniversary?"

She laughed. "No, that's not for another two weeks yet."

"I knew that… Yes, I did. Happiest day of my life." He kissed her again to prove it, only realizing as he ended the deep, sloppy kiss that his breath must reek of brandy.

But Fiona was looking at him in that magical way and smiling.

Lord, he loved her.

"*Happiest* day," he insisted, and kissed her yet again because she did not seem to mind that he was a little drunk, and willingly kissed him back with heartfelt sweetness. He gave her another kiss, this one tender. "What is it, love?"

"It has been *three* months, Rob."

He blinked.

"Three months since my last monthly courses," she explained as tears filled her eyes. "Rob, can it be possible? I had to tell you. I'm so excited and yet so afraid I might be mistaken."

He inhaled sharply. "How do you feel, Fiona? Any unsettled stomach issues?"

"Only a little. Nothing like Margaret experienced."

He shook his head, completely sober now. "Oh, love. Everyone is different. Whatever happens, we'll work through it together. It is early days yet, isn't it?"

She nodded. "And it might just be a mistake, just my being very late."

"No mistake. You have been looking particularly magical lately. Glowing. And your bosom…" He cupped a breast, holding it lightly to show her how it filled his hand more than usual. "Is it tender?"

She nodded again.

He laid her gently on her back and stretched out beside her, placing an arm under her shoulders with exquisite care and drawing her into his embrace. "I noticed, and yet dismissed the cues."

"Me too. Assuming there are any and I am not misreading everything."

"You aren't. Your body doesn't lie. Anyway, it doesn't matter. We are in this together no matter the outcome," he said with a soft growl, turning toward her to caress her cheek.

She nestled against him. "I love the way you look at me with your gorgeous panther eyes."

"How could I not? You'll always be my fairy princess." He kissed her softly on the lips, then grinned. Was it possible that chunk of lapis he'd kept in his undergarment drawer all this time had worked its magic?

He could hardly credit such myths. But what a miracle if Fiona truly carried his child. Just the possibility of it gave him a hope beyond imagination.

"Do you wonder what we'll have when we cross a panther with a fairy princess?"

Fiona's laughter was lilting, and she smiled at him. "Isn't the answer obvious?"

He shook his head, still feeling a little foggy. "Some guidance, please."

"You and me? Panther and fairy?"

He nodded. "And…"

"Starlight, Rob. Always starlight."

THE END

Also by Meara Platt

FARTHINGALE SERIES
My Fair Lily
The Duke I'm Going To Marry
Rules For Reforming A Rake
A Midsummer's Kiss
The Viscount's Rose
Earl of Hearts
The Viscount and the Vicar's Daughter
A Duke For Adela
Marigold and the Marquess
The Make-Believe Marriage
A Slight Problem With The Wedding
One Night With Tulip
If You Wished For Me
Never Dare A Duke
Capturing The Heart Of A Cameron

BOOK OF LOVE SERIES
The Look of Love
The Touch of Love
The Taste of Love
The Song of Love
The Scent of Love
The Kiss of Love
The Chance of Love
The Gift of Love
The Heart of Love
The Promise of Love
The Wonder of Love

The Journey of Love
The Treasure of Love
The Dance of Love
The Miracle of Love
The Hope of Love (novella)
The Dream of Love (novella)
The Remembrance of Love (novella)
All I Want For Christmas (novella)

MOONSTONE LANDING SERIES
Moonstone Landing (novella)
Moonstone Angel (novella)
The Moonstone Duke
The Moonstone Marquess
The Moonstone Major
The Moonstone Governess
The Moonstone Hero
The Moonstone Pirate

DARK GARDENS SERIES
Garden of Shadows
Garden of Light
Garden of Dragons
Garden of Destiny
Garden of Angels

SILVER DUKES
Cherish and the Duke
Moonlight and the Duke
Two Nights with the Duke
Snowfall and the Duke
Starlight and the Duke
Crash Landing on the Duke

LYON'S DEN
The Lyon's Surprise

Kiss of the Lyon
Lyon in the Rough

THE BRAYDENS
A Match Made In Duty
Earl of Westcliff
Fortune's Dragon
Earl of Kinross
Earl of Alnwick
Tempting Taffy
Aislin
Genalynn
Pearls of Fire*
*also in Pirates of Britannia series

DeWOLFE PACK ANGELS SERIES
Nobody's Angel
Kiss An Angel
Bhrodi's Angel

About the Author

Meara Platt is a USA Today bestselling author and an award winning, Amazon UK All-star with over seventy books published. Her favorite place in all the world is England's Lake District, which may not come as a surprise since many of her stories are set in that idyllic landscape, including her award winning, fantasy romance (romantasy) Dark Gardens series. If you'd like to learn more about the ancient Fae prophecy that is about to unfold in the Dark Gardens series, as well as Meara's lighthearted, international bestselling Regency romances in the Farthingale series, Book of Love series, and Silver Dukes series, or her more emotional Moonstone Landing series and Braydens series, please visit Meara's website at www.mearaplatt.com.

www.ingramcontent.com/pod-product-compliance
Lightning Source LLC
Chambersburg PA
CBHW072124300726
48975CB00003B/910